MACKINAC PASSAGE:
MYSTERY AT
ROUND ISLAND LIGHT

Robert A. Lytle

Illustrated
by Karen Howell

2648 Lapeer Rd.
Auburn Hills, MI   48326
(248) 475-4678
Fax (248) 475-9122
www.edcopublishing.com

First Printing 2001
Second Printing 2005

EDCO Publishing, Inc.
2648 Lapeer Road
Auburn Hills, Michigan 48326

Mackinac Passage: Mystery at Round Island Light is a work of
fiction and any resemblance to characters living or dead is
not intentional.

Library of Congress Control Number: 2002512388

ISBN-13: 978-0-9712692-3-1 (paperback)
ISBN-10: 0-9712692-3-8 (paperback)
ISBN-13: 978-0-9712692-0-0 (hard cover)
ISBN-10: 0-9712692-0-3 (hard cover)

Printed in the United States of America

ACKNOWLEDGEMENTS

As with the other Mackinac Passage stories, I wrote *Mystery at Round Island Light* with the help of many people. I am very fortunate to have met Skip Warp. Skip is a lifelong West Bluff summer resident who had many boyhood adventures with his friends on Round Island. Also, Skip's Mackinac neighbors, Dick and Linda Kughn provided the setting and incentive for some of the story's ideas.

In addition, I had several conversations with Pat Murray, whose family spans four generations on Mackinac soil. His great grandfather immigrated to Michigan from Ireland in 1838. I also spoke with Dale Gensman, the guiding force behind the Round Island Lighthouse's renovation. His father helped build the lighthouse over a century ago. Each person provided many inside accounts of life as it was on one of North America's most fascinating and historic places, Mackinac Island. Wes Maurer, Jr. provided several photos for my sister and illustrator to use for her sketches.

Longtime friends, Ken Johnson, Bill and Diane Ebinger, my wife, Candy and my son Ian, proofread early drafts and added much constructive criticism. Additionally, EDCO employees and friends Edna Stephens, Keith Cunningham and Linda McGarry added greatly in each of their areas of expertise.

Also, I wish to thank well-known author, William X. Kienzle and his wife/editor Javan, for their suggestions, encouragement and expertise into the nuances of the literary world.

Finally, I am deeply indebted to my sister Karen Lytle Howell who designed and drew the cover as well as the sketches for each chapter heading.

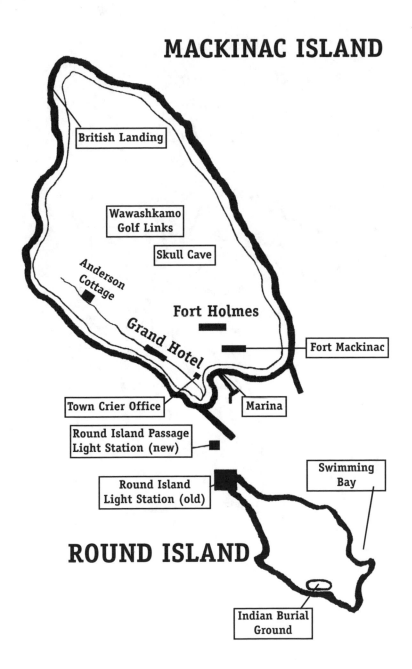

MACKINAC ISLAND

British Landing

Wawashkamo
Golf Links

Skull Cave

Anderson
Cottage

Fort Holmes

Grand Hotel

Fort Mackinac

Town Crier Office

Marina

Round Island Passage
Light Station (new)

Round Island
Light Station (old)

Swimming
Bay

ROUND ISLAND

Indian Burial
Ground

Ship Routes of ...
The Quince
and
The V.A. Frazier

The Quince — — — — — —
The V.A. Frazier — · — · —

Anderson's Spacious Veranda

CHAPTER 1
MORNING VIEW

Pete Jenkins stared out across the water. He rocked slowly in a brown wicker chair that glistened in the morning sun.

"Ever been over there?" he asked his new summer friend, Dan Hinken.

Both had their feet propped on the railing of the Andersons' spacious veranda. Dan's aunt and uncle's enormous cottage overlooked the Straits from Mackinac Island's fashionable West Bluff. Pete had been invited to stay with his new friends for the next week. He couldn't imagine anyone calling this thirty-room mansion a *cottage*. His family's cabin in the Snows was a cottage—two bedrooms, tiny kitchen, no electricity; its only running water came through the roof on rainy days.

"Please?" Dan asked politely. Dan's father was a wealthy Cincinnati doctor and for Dan, his aunt and uncle's summer home was nice, but nothing special.

"Have you ever been over to that lighthouse?" Pete rephrased.

1

"The old one on Round Island?" Dan asked.

Pete nodded.

"No, why?"

"I just wondered," Pete said. "It looks so strange—all by itself—like it's haunted or something. Does anyone live there?"

"I wouldn't think so," Dan answered. "When the new station was built off the Mackinac Island breakwater five years ago, they shut the old one down. Before that, a man had to stay on Round Island all the time. He lit the lamp at sundown, doused it at dawn and sounded the horn whenever fog rolled in—day or night."

"All year?" Pete asked.

"Sure," Dan said. "Except in the winter after the lakes froze. Then he'd come over here and stay in the village until the ice broke and freighters started moving again."

Several moments passed as the two boys stared out across the water. Dan's thoughts drifted from the old lighthouse to two yachts gliding silently toward Cheboygan. Pete kept his eyes on the decaying, red-and-white structure.

Finally Pete spoke up. "Did you ever *see* him?"

Dan turned to Pete. "Please?" he asked.

"The lighthouse keeper," Pete explained. "Did you ever see him?"

"You still on that?" Dan said with a laugh. "No, I never saw him. Not up close, at least. But I *do* remember he didn't like visitors—unless they had four legs or wings. He carried a scattergun everywhere he went and used it to shoo people away. He told them they were trespassing on government land and walked the whole island several times a day. If anybody tried to beach a boat any place on the island, he'd give 'em what for."

Pete's other new summer friend, Eddie Terkel,

2

pushed open the front screen door. He held it for Dan's twin sister Kate, who stepped onto the porch carrying a platter heaped high with warm Danish pastries, raspberry croissants and plump sticky buns. She set her breakfast offerings on a four-foot-wide wicker table. Eddie followed with a tray loaded with fresh fruit.

Eddie Terkel was Dan and Kate Hinken's neighbor both in Cincinnati and at their large, summer homes in the nearby Les Cheneaux Islands, or the Snows, as they were often called. The three had grown up as inseparable companions—sailing, skiing and partying with their elite circle of friends, running around the thirty-six islands in their speedboats, sloops and cruisers.

Although he had been coming to the Snows almost as long as they had, to the others Pete Jenkins was the new kid. He was the son of a small-town Michigan high school teacher and strictly by chance, a fairly close summer neighbor to these rich, southern Ohio resorters.

He was pretty ordinary, especially compared with the Cincinnati Row crowd. But as different as he was from them, they accepted him as an equal and invited him to all their social events. In return, Pete introduced them to his favorite, although somewhat less glamorous pastime—fishing. For Pete, the exchange was more than fair.

That summer, the four met with some sort of danger at almost every turn. Pete's role had slowly become that of rescuer for his thrill-seeking companions, who sought out adventure with reckless abandon.

The screen door sprang shut, slapping the pine frame with the same resounding clap it had made since the huge summer home was built in 1895. Such magnificent cottages along the bluffs were as much a part of the island's charm as were the rhythmic, clip-clomping beats of passing horse-drawn carriages, the sweet, warm aroma

3

from village fudge shops and the cool, fragrant breezes that swept through the cedars and the gleaming white Fort Mackinac walls.

"You guys can bring out the rest of the breakfast," Kate said, pulling two chairs to the table. "Mrs. Odom has everything set in the kitchen. Aunt and Uncle aren't up yet, so we're on our own."

Pete and Dan hopped out of their rockers and headed for the door. Pete took a last look across the water at the deserted lighthouse before he disappeared inside. He followed Dan through the living room, dining area and long hallway to the kitchen. He glanced at the electric clock above the stove. It was five minutes to seven.

Normally, Pete wasn't an early riser, unless the bass were hitting, but when Dan tapped at his bedroom door, he got up, dressed and hurried downstairs almost before he realized what he was doing.

Mrs. Odom, an elderly black woman and one of eight house servants, poured milk into a crystal pitcher and set it alongside four goblets. She had held an honored position in the Anderson family for fifty years, hired as a nanny to George Anderson when he was only a baby. Mrs. Odom handed the silver platter to Pete. On another tray, she set silverware, linen napkins, china plates and a pitcher of juice with four more crystal tumblers and handed that tray to Dan.

"You boys be careful now," she instructed as she opened the kitchen door for them.

Pete retraced his steps down the hall, past the dining area and into the living room. Dan held the screen door open and Pete stepped over the threshold onto the porch. He set his tray on the table next to the fruit and pastries.

The four filled their plates, sat down and looked out across one of the most spectacular views in the entire

4

Great Lakes. A light, westerly breeze carried across the top of Lake Michigan, through the narrow Straits of Mackinac and onto Lake Huron. A gigantic American flag flapped occasionally as it hung from the pole that jutted straight out from the porch.

The early morning sun hadn't yet chased away the northern night's chill, but Pete knew it would soon be warm enough for the shorts and T-shirt he was wearing. He settled into his chair with his hot-buttered Danish and pulpy, fresh orange juice.

Soon, his eyes shifted back to the old lighthouse. While the others chatted about how they had gotten through the previous day in one piece, Pete became lost in thought about the lonely structure on the tip of the neighboring island. *Why had the keeper tried to run people off?* he wondered. *What was he trying to protect?—or hide? What's on the rest of the island?* Pete *had* to go there.

The handsome old lighthouse was inviting yet spooky, stately though crumbling, nearby yet inaccessible. How one place could be so many things all at once only made it more alluring.

"Could the guy still be living there?" Pete asked.

Dan glanced at Pete to see what he was referring to. He saw that Pete was staring at the old signal station. "Oh . . . uh, I don't know. Probably not. It's not his job anymore." He looked over to Eddie and Kate. "Pete and I were talking about the Round Island Lighthouse."

Eddie rolled his eyes and went back to his hot pastry. Kate looked up in interest, catching Dan's attention as she took a sip of her juice.

"You're not thinking of going over there," Eddie said to Kate, noticing her glance in Dan's direction.

Kate hopped to her feet. "Oh, let's do!" she said.

5

"I've always wanted to explore the place. We could make a day of it—take a packed lunch. It would be great fun."

Eddie shook his head slowly. "Not this sailor," he said.

"Come on, Eddie. Why not?" Kate asked.

"Well, for one thing," Eddie drawled in his southern Ohio accent, "if the old guy *is* still guarding his government property—whether it's his job or not—I'm not sure I'd like to test his aim."

"Get real, Eddie," Kate said. "He's probably tending another lighthouse a hundred miles away."

Pete leaned forward in his chair. "How can we find out?" he asked.

"We could go to the Coast Guard station," Dan said. "They're in charge of the new light. They could tell us."

"But they wouldn't know about the old keeper," Eddie argued. "Not for sure, anyway."

"I bet Mr. Dufina would," Kate suggested. "Besides, we've got to return his book."

"Let's go ask him," Dan agreed, moving to the door.

"Right now?" Eddie said. "It's barely seven o'clock."

"Not everyone sleeps in like Aunt and Uncle," said Kate. She had a look in her eyes like the light on a runaway train. Once she'd made up her mind, she was an irresistible force—nothing could slow her down.

Eddie recognized the sign. "All right then, but we're not sailing over in the *Griffin*. The shore's too rocky. You can see that from here."

"We'll take Uncle George's dinghy," Dan said, siding with his twin sister as he almost always did. They thought alike—even had dreams at night that often foretold danger. The two could be positively spooky. "It

6

can seat four," he added, "and it's got a motor so we won't even have to row."

"You want to cross the shipping channel in a *dinghy*?" Eddie laughed. "You can't be serious! Do you know how strong the current is? And what happens if the motor conks out? Those seven-hundred-foot freighters come through going upwards of fifteen knots. Even if the captain saw us floundering around he couldn't stop. We'd go under her bow and be chopped up in her props like sausage in a meat grinder."

"Oh, Eddie," Kate said. "You're beginning to sound like Pete. You've got us drowned and dead before we're even off Aunt and Uncle's porch."

"Kate's right," Dan said to Eddie. "Let's not get ahead of ourselves. First, we'll return Mr. Dufina's book and find out about the old lighthouse keeper. We can worry about crossing to Round Island later."

View From Porch To Round Island

CHAPTER 2
THE LIGHTHOUSE KEEPER

The four friends carried their trays into the kitchen and hurried out back to the carriage barn. They grabbed their bikes and pedaled past the Grand Hotel down the long hill into town. After coasting to Emerson Dufina's home on French Lane, they set their kickstands and walked up to the old man's front porch.

Dan put an ear to the door and held his finger to his lips. "Hold on a sec," he said as he listened. "There, I can hear a radio. He must be up." He cranked the handle on the doorbell. In moments the carpenter appeared and invited his young visitors inside.

"We're here to return your book," Kate said.

The grizzled craftsman eyed the four fresh faces. "That's not all you want," he said with a smile peeking from between his gnarled, grey beard and mustache. "I can see a heap more tomfoolery in your eyes than that, or I'm no judge o' humankind."

"Well, okay," Dan said. "We also wanted to ask you about the Round Island Lighthouse."

"Uh-huh," Emerson Dufina said with a grunt.

9

"And just what would you like to know?"

"Whatever you can tell us," Kate said, "like when it was built, who was the keeper, where he went—stuff like that."

Mr. Dufina stared at his eager guests then sat back in his chair and tugged at his beard. "I was here when Jesse Muldoon first lit that lighthouse lamp back in 1895," he said, "and in all those fifty-some years he never failed to warn a ship during the blackest night or fiercest gale. Even during the great November storms of 1913 and 1940, when the entire Great Lakes became a graveyard for hundreds of men and ships—even then, ol' Jesse stood his watch. It was a sorry day five years ago when he doused its flame for the last time."

"What became of him?" Dan asked.

"Nobody's rightly sure," Mr. Dufina said, shaking his head. "The Coast Guard told him he could work here on Mackinac doing maintenance on the new light, but he didn't want any part of that. Not in the summers anyhow. 'Too dad-gum many people,' is what he told me. He wanted a job at a different harbor, but all the Great Lakes lighthouses were being shut down or automated. Jesse was pretty old—in his eighties, I guess.

After he refused the job here, he just up and disappeared. Some people think he's living over there on the island even now, but I don't know how he could be. Tom Willis—he works at the coal dock—he says he saw a light in the tower almost five years ago, the first winter she was closed. Everyone around here knows the story. It was mid-January during a terrible cold snap. Tom would swear to this day that he saw the lighthouse lamp flicker on and off for the better part of a minute. He had half of us believin' it."

"Didn't anyone check it out?" Kate asked.

"Not right then, not as cold as it was. No one was

10

that curious. Some Coast Guard men walked across on the ice a week late but they said there was no sign anyone had been inside—no ashes in the stove, nothing at all. And the place was sealed up tight. My guess is Tom just saw the sun reflecting off the lighthouse windows."

"If Mr. Muldoon *is* still there, what could he be living on?" Eddie asked. "Is there any game on the island?—any place to grow a garden?"

"That's just it," Emerson said. "There's no way he could live off the land. Even the old Indian tribes never stayed, not for long, at least. The Odawas have an ancient burial ground there. *Min-nis-ais*, that's what they called it, means Little Island—it's only about three miles around. It's a sacred place for them, but livable?—I don't think it ever was. No, I believe Jesse has left these parts forever. Why do you want to know?"

"We were thinking we might go over," said Dan.

Eddie spoke up. "But if there's any chance of getting shot at, we'll find some other way to spend our time."

Emerson Dufina threw his head back and laughed. "That old story is still going around," he said, a smile filling his face.

"What do you mean?" Dan said. "It's not true about Mr. Muldoon scaring people off with his shotgun?"

"No, it's true, all right," Emerson said, still grinning. "But he only did it once and then simply because some treasure hunter came up here from down below—Detroit or somewhere. The man started digging around in the Indian burial ground. When Jesse saw what he was doing, Jesse marched him over to the lighthouse at gunpoint and sent him packing with a couple of blasts from his old over-and-under, double-barrel shotgun. Everyone here on Mackinac stopped what they were doing and stared at the two men on the nearby island."

11

"Really?" Kate asked. "You could hear it all the way over here?"

"Oh, yeah," said Mr. Dufina. "I was up by the fort and it was like a cannon had gone off. Everyone watched the treasure hunter get in his rowboat and hightail it back here. When he pulled ashore at Biddle Point he was met by a huge crowd of folks. I hurried all the way down the hill to be there. We all wanted to know what the devil had happened to set Jesse off like that. All the man said was that the lighthouse keeper was a raving lunatic and that he'd shot at him for no reason at all. It wasn't till the next winter that Jesse told me what had happened. By then the story of the crazy ol' Round Island lighthouse keeper was pretty well all over the Great Lakes."

"So, no one ever went there again?" Dan asked.

"Not for the last thirty years," Mr. Dufina said. "It didn't hurt that a body could stand here and watch Jesse carrying that shotgun over his shoulder as he made his rounds of the island."

"Let's get back to Aunt and Uncle's," Kate said, getting up. "Thanks for lending us the book, Mr. Dufina."

The four started for the door.

"Be careful," Mr. Dufina said with a wink.

Dan looked in surprise at the old man. "Of what?" he asked.

"Well, if you should head over to Round Island," he said with a sly grin, "remember, I never told you Jesse Muldoon *isn't* there—or that he still ain't totin' that ol' over-and-under, watchin' for uninvited visitors."

"I don't like what the current is doing."

CHAPTER 3
THE CROSSING

The four friends pumped their bikes as far up Grand Hill as they could then hopped off and pushed them along the service road behind the landmark hotel. After catching her breath, Kate said, "This will be such fun. We'll ask Mrs. Odom to make some sandwiches and we'll take them to Round Island in the wicker picnic basket."

"We can trap a bunch of crabs on the beach and boil them like lobsters," Dan continued. "It'll be a real feast."

"I still want to know how we'll get across," Eddie said.

Pete followed the others, wishing he'd kept his earlier thoughts about the lighthouse to himself. His interest in the subject had dimmed about the time he learned they would be going over in a dinghy and they might get chopped up in a seven-hundred-foot meat grinder. What little enthusiasm that remained totally failed him when the discussion got around to being shot at by some deranged lighthouse keeper.

It was bad enough when he was the only one who recognized danger. But when Eddie was uneasy about something, then it *really* made him nervous. Eddie Terkel, who was powerful enough to blast a softball out of any park, would be no match for a fifteen-thousand-ton, all-engines-full-ahead freighter. Eddie had sailed these waters often, so he knew better than Dan or Kate how the current ran.

Pete had never thought about a current. These were the Great *Lakes*, not the Great *Rivers*. All the lakes Pete had ever seen didn't have any current. They were like puddles—they just sat there. But then he realized that all the Great Lakes flowed eventually into the Atlantic Ocean. If they *flowed*, there *must* be a current. The Great Lakes really *was* one huge river. Water going through a narrow place like the Straits of Mackinac was probably moving pretty fast. Anyone trying to cross it in a dinghy powered by a one-horse motor could get themselves in a whole mess of trouble in a very short hurry.

Kate led the group into the Andersons' kitchen where Mrs. Odom was putting away the kids' breakfast plates. It was nearly eight o'clock and there was still no sign of Aunt and Uncle.

"We're going for a picnic, Mrs. Odom," Dan said. "We'll be back for dinner."

"I'll make some sandwiches for you," she said cheerfully. "Lan' sakes, where y'all off to this time?"

"Just on the island," Dan replied. He was careful not to say *which* island—no sense getting Aunt and Uncle in a stir. One more misadventure like the last one and they would never be invited back. Besides, what could happen? They were just going on a picnic.

In minutes the four were pedaling toward the marina. They flew down Hoban Lane onto Huron Avenue and past the smaller hotels, fudge shops and gift stores. Only a few early risers ambled along the quiet sidewalks and the street was still wet from its earlier hosing. The first ferry would not arrive for another hour, bringing hordes of people that would transform this quaint, sleepy

14

village into one of bustling activity.

Dan hopped from his bike and led the others to Mr. Anderson's dinghy tied to the stern of the *M·I·S·T*, his sixty-foot yacht.

Pete looked at the small dory. No way could four people fit into that. It was smaller than his aluminum fishing boat, which even he referred to as the *Tiny Tin*. And with *this* they would cross to Round Island? Not likely.

Dan moved down the boarding ladder and unsnapped the canvas cover. He rolled it back, revealing a sturdily built dinghy with a mint-condition, pre-WWI Evinrude motor. There was not a drop of water on the sparkling, varnished floorboards. The small boat bounced easily in the light waves of the sheltered harbor. Dan folded the tarp and stuffed it under the stern seat.

Pete stared at the tiny craft. There was room for four people, but only if nobody breathed. Kate followed Dan nimbly down the ladder and stepped into the center of the boat. It barely quivered. Eddie was next. As agile as he was, the boat wobbled precariously from side to side before he grabbed the dock and steadied her. He sat in the stern next to Dan, leaving room for Pete beside Kate in the bow.

All three looked up at Pete. Pete peered at the water line on the outside of the dinghy. The boat was only inches from swamping. *Oh, man. This would be awful,* Pete thought, *sinking right here at the dock.*

"Are you sure about this?" he asked, staring at Dan.

"Sure, I'm sure," Dan said. "We've taken her all the way around Mackinac before—in a lot rougher water than this, too."

"How long ago was that?" Pete probed.

"Two, maybe three years," Dan said with a shrug. "I don't remember. Why?"

"Do you happen to know how much you *weighed* back then?"

"Come on, Pete," Kate taunted from the bow. "Don't be such a worrywart." She moved over another inch and nodded to the seat Pete would take beside her.

Pete looked into her beautiful, smiling face. The chance to please her was too great to pass up. He would do *anything* for her. He moved toward the ladder.

"Don't forget the picnic basket," Eddie said.

Pete glanced behind him and lifted the wicker case. He mentally added its weight to his own and calculated its effect upon the already overburdened boat. He looked at the waves lapping at the gunwales. He glanced at the unoccupied seat and at Kate next to it. Without so much as another blink, he dropped the basket to Eddie and stepped down the ladder into the dinghy.

Kate put her arm around him and gave him a squeeze. "Oh, Pete, I just knew you'd come. Everything will be fine. You'll see."

Pete was so glad he had ignored his better judgment. His face grew hot as she snuggled closer to him. He turned his eyes to Dan, who was winding the pull cord around the tiny engine's starting mechanism. He watched Dan, but his thoughts were on Kate.

"Shove off, Eddie," Dan said as he yanked the handle. The motor broke the silence with a soft putt-putt-putt and the overloaded dinghy moved out into the bay.

Pete could imagine what they must look like from shore. It was a disaster waiting to happen. The very first wave in the open water would send them to their death. For years to come parents would cite this day as a warning to children who didn't ask for advice before starting off on a hazardous journey.

Dan steered the dinghy around the Arnold dock without incident and Pete began to relax. He looked astern

16

over the top of the old motor and surveyed the shoreline of the picturesque village. Little by little the town was awakening to another day that would be memorable to thousands of visitors—some who would see Mackinac for the first time and others who would marvel at its beauty for the ten-thousandth.

Pete became increasingly aware of a cold spray chilling the back of his neck. He glanced to the side and realized that the dinghy had come to the end of the west breakwater. He turned farther and looked over the bow. They were moving into the shipping channel. Just ahead was the new, automatic light station—a steel and concrete contraption erected, not on land, like a proper lighthouse, but stationed, sterile and uninhabitable, in the open water. Even though there was little wind, Pete could see a powerful current swirling at the barren structure's corners.

Dan kept the bow pointed toward the old lighthouse on Round Island, the little engine at full speed. Suddenly, Pete realized that the boat was no longer moving.

"I don't like what this current is doing," Eddie said. "We're not making any headway. Bring her around, Dan. Take her back to harbor."

Pete noticed a look of concern on Dan's face. Dan turned the rudder and the dinghy spun halfway around, pointing toward the west breakwater. Dan's expression became one of dread as they made no progress in that direction either. "What's happening?" Dan asked in alarm. "We can't go forward *or* back!"

"We're stuck in the current!" Kate screamed.

"Head for the new light station!" Eddie directed. "If we can't reach that and hold it till we get help, we could be swept out into Lake Huron! No telling where we'd end up."

Dan turned the tiller again, this time swinging the

17

boat into the current. For several moments nothing happened. They seemed to be caught in a whirlpool. Then, slowly the boat inched toward the steel structure sixty feet away.

Pete glanced from the light station to the Mackinac Island shoreline. Churning straight for their bow, the first Arnold Line ferry of the day bore down on them.

"Dan!" Pete yelled, pointing to the passenger boat.

"Oh, no! We'll never make it!" Kate shrieked. "She's going to swamp us!"

"Turn toward Round Island, Dan!" Eddie yelled. "Maybe her wake will push us out of this current."

Dan whipped the rudder another ninety degrees, aiming the dinghy away from the path of the ferry and in the direction of the Round Island Lighthouse.

The huge Arnold boat plowed toward them, pushing a wall of water from its bow. As it swept past the new light station, all three hundred of her passengers waved happily at the four terror-stricken teens sitting in the tiny boat.

The bow wave rushed toward them. Pete felt the forward thrust as it pushed them ahead. The dinghy rose high on the rolling wave and then settled back onto the flat surface of the calm Straits water. They had gained a few yards toward their goal.

"Hold on everyone!" Eddie yelled. "Here comes the big one!"

Pete looked behind the dinghy. The first real breaker was crashing at them like a tidal wave.

"Lean forward!" Dan yelled.

The stern came out of the water and the motor whined with a high-pitched wail, its propeller spinning wildly in the air. The four teens clutched the gunwales as they huddled together in the bow.

The dinghy shot forward, riding the six-foot crest.

The wave continued until the small boat stood momentarily on top of the water, resting like a bobber on the sea.

"Lean back!" Dan called. Suddenly the bow tipped almost straight up and the stern dropped to the trough of the wave. The propeller bore into the water with a groan.

Pete whirled in his seat. In all directions green water, six feet higher than his head, surged past the boat.

"Move forward! Here comes the next one!" Dan called.

The boat rose into the air. It rode neither as high nor as far as with the first wave. Pete knew instantly that the worst was over. He glanced ahead. They were almost to Round Island. The boat settled down on the back side of the wave. The lake, once again, was calm.

"We certainly made the best of that," Eddie said.

The Round Island Lighthouse stood at the tip end of the narrow spit of land twenty yards away. The motor putt-putted softly, pushing the dinghy toward it. Pete looked over the side into the greenish-blue water. Rock formations the size of cabins lay twenty feet below. The bottom rose quickly as they approached the shoreline.

"Watch for rocks, Pete," Dan said. "This isn't as sandy as it looks from across the way."

Pete guided Dan around some boulders that appeared to be closer to the surface in the crystalline water than they really were. Finally, the dinghy ground to a stop on the sand-and-pebble beach.

"That was fun," Eddie said sarcastically as he followed Pete and Kate onto the shore. "I hope it won't take another miracle to get us back."

"Let's worry about that later," Kate said, her eyes darting about at the new surroundings. "I want to explore this island."

The Round Island Lighthouse

CHAPTER 4
ROUND ISLAND

Dan grabbed the bow line and pulled the dory over the smooth, flat pebbles high onto the beach. He hurried to reach the others, who had gone ahead and were staring up at the Round Island Lighthouse from its base.

"It's a lot bigger than it looks from your aunt and uncle's front porch," Pete said.

"The tower must be fifty feet high," Dan agreed.

Kate began to walk around the outside. "Let's see if we can get in," she said. "Here's the door." She turned the knob as the boys came to her side. "No luck, it's locked."

"Let's try a window," Dan suggested. The four continued around the entire brick building, but every opening was shuttered and bolted.

"Oh, well," Kate said, "it was fun just seeing it up close. I wonder what will become of it now that it's not being used anymore."

"It will probably fall apart like the boathouses in the Snows when they're not cared for," Eddie said. "A few more winters and nobody will know it was ever here."

"That's too bad," said Pete. "Someone ought to take care of it."

"Like who?" Eddie asked.

"I don't know," Pete said. "But somebody should. It's too neat a place to let it just crumble away."

"Maybe so," Eddie said, "but that's the way it is. If it doesn't fatten someone's wallet, then whoosh, it's gone. Let's see what's on the rest of the island."

Soon, the four were hiking around the shoreline, taking a clockwise route along the beach. The midmorning sun had chased the chill from the air.

"What are we looking for?" Pete asked as he picked up a flat stone. He turned and fired it sidearm onto the calm water. He counted five long skips and four pitter-patters before the pebble sank into the depths.

"Good one," Dan said. "But they're not `skips' and `pitter-patters.' They're `ducks, drakes and ducklings.' My turn. Watch this." He found a perfectly disc-shaped stone, flipped it like a quarter into his right hand and then whipped it into the bay. It skimmed along the water, skipping six times before sailing high into the air and splashing into the lake. "I won," he said, smiling at Pete.

"No way! You didn't get any pitter-patters or ducklings or whatever you call them," Pete said as he searched the ground for another suitable rock.

"Ducklings don't count," Dan answered. "Just the ducks and drakes. Everyone knows that. And I got six of them."

"Come on guys, you can skip stones on Mackinac. I want to find the Indian burial ground," Kate said, looking away from the shore and peering inland toward the dense island forest.

"Any idea where it is?" Pete asked.

22

"Not really," Kate said, "but if we find a clearing or a pathway into the island through this underbrush, we'll take it and see where it goes."

"If the Indians brought their dead here by canoe," Dan said, "it would make sense that they would land on a sandy shoreline."

"The bay up ahead seems to be a likely spot," said Pete.

The four made their way to a partially sheltered cove. "It's protected all right, but it's too rocky for a canoe to land here," Eddie said.

"And the forest is even more dense than back there," Pete added.

"Let's keep going," Eddie suggested. "There's got to be a break in the woods somewhere."

Dan and Kate had been walking quietly. Finally, Kate spoke up. "Didn't Mr. Dufina say that the Indian burial ground was on the southwest part of Round Island?"

"I don't remember him saying that," said Eddie.

"Well, that's where I picture it," she said, "but for the life of me, I don't know why."

Dan stepped in front of Kate and stopped, staring her straight in the eye. "It wasn't Mr. Dufina who told us that," Dan said uneasily. "It was in a dream, Kate. I didn't want to say anything about it until you did, but we must have had the same dream last night. And you know what *that* means. It was just like a week ago when Miss Fisher's house almost burned down. We had a dream that night, too. Only this time my dream didn't make any sense, so I didn't try to wake you up. What was yours about, Kate?"

"It was really scary," Kate said, looking out into the shallow bay. "The four of us were walking in the dead of night. We were here on Round Island—on the southwest shore. We could see a fire blazing inland

23

behind a stand of cedars. There was a break in the forest and we started up a sharp bank. We came to a clearing and found three men sitting in shadows. Firelight flickered red in their faces. When they saw us, they hollered and ran toward us—that's when I woke up."

"Did you recognize them?" Dan asked anxiously.

Kate closed her eyes. "No, only that they were very angry we had interrupted their ritual or whatever it was." She opened her eyes and looked at her brother. "Is that what yours was about?"

"Close enough," Dan replied.

Eddie stared at the twins. "You *both* dreamed about Round Island *last* night?" he breathed. "That was before we even thought about coming here."

"Maybe that's why when Pete asked about the lighthouse at breakfast, we were so eager to go," Dan said.

"I hate to bring this up," Pete said, "but usually when you both have a dream like this, doesn't something really bad happen?—a fire breaks out or a building blows up? Nothing very exciting seems to be going on, except maybe for our trip across in the dinghy."

"You're right, Pete," Dan agreed. "It could be that the two dreams don't really mean anything this time. But it's odd that we both pictured the burial ground on the southwest shore of the island."

"Maybe you saw it in Mr. Dufina's book," Eddie said. "Anyway, around that next point will be the southwest shore. If we find an opening into the island, then I'd say there might be something to it."

The four continued along the beach and around the southern tip of the island. They hadn't gone a hundred yards when Dan noticed a small opening in the forest wall.

"Check this out," he said.

24

Kate gasped. "This is just like what I saw—only it's daytime. Come on, let's go in."

"What if we see someone?—those three guys in your dream?" Pete said nervously. "We'd better be ready to get out of there fast."

Dan led the way up the steep embankment of twisted roots and jagged rocks through a narrow break in the cedar underbrush. He walked past a fire pit and stood in a clearing about the size of a softball infield. All around it were trees and bushes and thick brush, but within the oval, nothing grew but moss and sparse weeds.

"This must be the burial place," Kate whispered. "Look there, between the rocks. The ground is sunken a few inches. And there. And over there." She pointed to several spots, each roughly the shape of a human body. Grey, lichen-encrusted stones covered the shallow pits.

"This is really strange," Dan said. "Everything is exactly like in my dream except it was all dug up—like a pack of animals had torn into every grave."

"I don't know about you," Pete said as he inched away from the others toward the shore, "but I don't think we belong here. Let's get back to the boat."

"And I'm hungry," Eddie said, moving along with Pete. "Let's have our picnic."

The Warning

CHAPTER 5
WARNING

As the four followed the rocky shoreline toward the lighthouse, Kate spoke up. "How do you feel, Pete? You looked a little pale back there."

"Better now," Pete said. "That Indian cemetery gave me the heebie-jeebies—especially with you two talking about your weird dreams."

Kate squeezed Pete's hand. "Eddie is probably right," she said. "There's really no reason to think that something bad is going to happen. Let's get this picnic started. You three can pull some of those driftwood logs together to sit on and I'll get the basket from the boat."

"The wind is picking up a bit," Eddie said, looking into the shipping channel. "The sooner we start back, the better. It was tricky enough coming across with no wind."

"Give me a hand with this plank, Pete," Dan said. "We'll lay it across these boulders and make a table out of it."

From the shore came a shout. "Come here, guys!" Kate yelled. "Hurry!"

"What's the matter?" Eddie called back.

"Something has gotten into our picnic basket!"

she answered.

"You're kidding!" Pete said. "What could have done that?"

The three boys dropped their boards and ran to Kate. The wicker chest was turned over on the shore. Its top was thrown open and food was scattered all over the beach. Plates were smashed on the rocks and napkins were flapping in the light breeze. All four stared open-mouthed at the litter that was once their lunch.

"Raccoons?" Eddie asked.

Dan shook his head. "I don't think so."

"Could'a been skunks or porcupines," Pete suggested. "They're all over my end of Big LaSalle. We toss our leftovers behind the cottage after dinner and they're always gone by the time I hit the outhouse before crawling in the sack."

"No," Dan answered. "Not skunks or raccoons or porcupines. They couldn't have knocked the basket out of the boat."

"A bear maybe?" Eddie said glancing quickly around him.

Dan again shook his head. "A bear would have eaten the food."

Kate leaned into the boat and picked a sheet of paper from the bow. She stared at it for a moment. "How about a person?" She handed the note to her brother. Dan read the message and shot glances in all directions—at the lighthouse, along the shoreline, into the woods.

"What's it say?" Pete asked.

Dan looked back at the message written in smudgy, bold pencil strokes. "It says, `Get off this island now! Don't come back!'"

"I don't suppose the guy bothered to sign it," Eddie said, looking over Dan's shoulder.

"No and there's no return address or RSVP either,"

Dan answered sarcastically.

"The man needs to brush up on his etiquette," Kate added.

"Maybe so," Eddie said. "But now is not the time to teach him."

"Do you think it could be kids?" Pete asked.

"Not a chance," Dan answered. "This isn't a childish prank. Whoever wrote that note is dead serious. I'd like to know who it is and why he did it."

"Whoa, Dan," Eddie said, stepping in, "you're letting your imagination run away with you. Let's think about this. Who could care *that* much about this worthless little island?"

"How about the old lighthouse keeper?" said Pete.

"Oh, yeah, I'd forgotten him," Eddie said.

"Well, whoever it is," Pete said, "I say we don't stick around to find out."

"Right," Eddie agreed, "and with this breeze, we'd better hurry."

Dan stared again at the lighthouse. He concentrated on the boarded-up lower windows, the door and then the thick glass sections high in the tower. "Okay," he said, "let's pack up and go."

The four gathered what remained of their picnic supplies and boarded the tiny dinghy. Dan pulled the starter cord and the boat chugged away from Round Island.

———

At the very peak of the lighthouse, high above the picnic site, two squinty eyes were fixed on a small boat carrying three boys and a girl across the narrow channel toward Mackinac Island.

———

For the return trip, Dan guided the *M·I·S·T's* dinghy on a diagonal course across the powerful Straits until they were safely back in the yacht harbor.

"What are we going to tell your aunt and uncle?" Pete asked.

"We might have to ease into the part about taking Uncle's dinghy to Round Island," Kate said.

"And how will we explain the broken dishes?" Pete added.

"Don't worry about that," Kate said. "They're just cheap picnic ware."

Pete was no judge of such things, but he was pretty sure those dishes were better than his parents' best Sunday dinner china. His mom would never let him take dishes *that* good on a picnic.

Dan pulled the Evinrude's throttle from *Full* to *Stop*, bringing the dinghy to the *M·I·S·T's* stern. He spoke for the first time since leaving Round Island. "I say we nose around town and see what we can find. Something is going on over there that someone doesn't want anyone to know about. Whoever broke up our party must have had a pretty good reason to try to scare us away."

Pete immediately noted Dan's words, " . . . try to scare us away." Pete didn't think there was any *try* to it. He had been scared away. Hadn't the others, too? What was with these kids? He slowly followed Kate up the ladder to the dock.

"Let's start at the <u>Town Crier</u>," Kate said as Dan snapped the canvas cover over the top of the small boat.

"And ask who, the editor?" Eddie said with a laugh.

"No," Dan said, nodding to his sister. "Great idea, Kate. We'll ask Ginny Lind, the editor's daughter. You two have been friends for years. Didn't you help her deliver papers the summer I broke my leg?"

"Yes," Kate answered. "I stayed here with Aunt and Uncle the month you were in the hospital. Ginny and

30

I were together practically the whole time hanging around the <u>Town Crier</u> office. I heard things that never would get printed."

"I'm starved," Dan said. "Let's go to the cottage and have lunch. We'll call Ginny from there."

Dan finished tying the dinghy to the stern of the *M·I·S·T* and the four started to the West Bluff. As they pumped their bikes up the Grand Hotel hill, Pete got to thinking how quickly things had changed since he met his new friends. In all the previous summers, the most exciting part of his entire vacation might be to find his way to the outhouse on a dark night—hardly a subject he could write about in his "What I Did This Summer" essay. This year, with his new friends, never a day went by without something major happening.

Why, just that morning he had been sitting on the Anderson porch, wondering what was on that tiny island across the way. In less than five hours, he had discovered more about it than he'd ever cared to—enough to know that he never wanted to go back. But he'd been with his new friends long enough to realize that wouldn't be an option. They simply couldn't sit still when even a hint of adventure came their way. Now once again, they were poking their noses into someone else's business—and Pete had a dreadful feeling it would come to no good.

Irish Eyes

CHAPTER 6
IRISH EYES

Nine months earlier, in a nearby part of Lake Huron, three freezing cold and bone-tired fishermen struggled to remain aboard their small commercial trawler. The iron-gray November sky was featureless from one horizon to the other. A savage gale pitched and rolled their vessel in and out of the clutches of what could be a swift and final voyage—one that would take them to the depths forever. Wind-driven sheets of stinging rain pelted the *Irish Eyes* and its three mariners.

"Haul in the nets!" Buck Meesley yelled over the howling wind. "We're runnin' low on gas!"

The two mates glanced at their captain. Without a word they began to crank the long, heavily weighted lines into the boat. Buck fought to keep the trawler pointed into the wind. Yard after yard of net came aboard with practically no fish in the tender to show for their efforts. This trip, like all others that season, was a bust.

"This is the worst!" Herman LeRoux yelled to the man at the wheel. "I ain't ever goin' out in this ol' tub again."

"*If* we make it in," Buck Meesley, the biggest and burliest of the three bellowed. He gripped the ship's wheel and wrestled it from side to side as the boat wallowed with each gigantic swell. "Besides, with no fish to sell, that rat-faced banker will have sole title to the *Irish Eyes* and I won't have nothin' to say about it. This trip could have saved our tails, but we needed a big haul. What few lakers we brung in wouldn't feed that miserable land shark his breakfast."

"What are we gonna do, Buck?" Herman asked.

"Without a boat? I dunno. Maybe go downstate. Work in some blast furnace somewheres," Buck answered.

"You ain't gettin' out that easy," the third man snarled. Sam Moilanen clutched a handhold on the port side of the bridge where he normally acted as first mate, checking the charts and compass for Buck. "Three years ago you talked Herman an' me into workin' for you and I ain't gonna let you walk away without payin'. You owe us, Buck, an' when we get back to port, we're gonna cash in equal-like."

"It didn't take much convincin', as I recall," Buck said. "I didn't *make* you work for me, eh? B'sides, you couldn't have gotten no job with nobody else. Look at you two. Who'd take either one of ya?"

"Mebbe not," Sam said, "but at least we wouldn't be in the fix we're in now."

"Okay, fine by me," Buck Meesley said, spinning the wheel to starboard as the bow slammed into the next comber. "You wanna be partners? I'll be glad to share my losses with you two boneheads. That banker can have three hides to take his money out of instead of just mine. And if the *Irish Eyes* don't cover our debts, we can *all* go to jail together."

"You serious?" Herman LeRoux said. "We could

34

get *time*?"

"You still wanna be in?" Buck taunted.

"It ain't right," Sam Moilanen muttered. "When guys bust their tails like we done, they're supposed to git somethin' for it."

"It don't always work that way an' you know it," Buck said. "Leastwise not in the fishin' trade. You guys go below—take a snooze. If we don't make it into harbor before sundown, I'll need some fresh eyes to find the buoys, or we may not make it in at all."

Buck's two mates turned and bumped their way down a two-step companionway into a cluttered galley. A week's worth of dirty pots, pans and dishes rattled in the sink as the two men stumbled along the narrow passage to their hammocks in the bow. Each rolled into his makeshift bed and pulled a soggy blanket over himself. Soon, they were swinging to the rhythm of the storm-tossed boat, snoring away as only seasoned sailors can under such miserable conditions.

Fatal Fire

CHAPTER 7
THE CHRISTMAS PRESENT

Sam Moilanen, Buck Meesley and Herman LeRoux had grown up like the Lost Boys in *Peter Pan*. The only difference was that they didn't have Peter or Wendy to guide them through the rough spots. These boys were born in the tiny fishing village of Little Perch Bay in Michigan's eastern Upper Peninsula. They entered the world on three consecutive days in three adjacent shanties along a two-track dirt road on the edge of town.

From the very beginning the three boys were nothing more than a bother to their parents and community—a population afflicted by a disastrous economy. What little prosperity Little Perch Bay had once known was now lost through the stripping of the pine forests and the overfishing of the lake trout.

The first of the three, Herman LeRoux, was of French and Native American parentage. He was short and stocky like his French papa, Jacques LeRoux. He had coal black hair and dark, copper-colored skin like his Odawa mother, Wintemoyeh. His face and neck were pocked and inflamed by the constant contact of his long, oily hair. His teeth were crooked and rotting, with the exception of the two front ones, which were completely missing knocked out by Buck Meesley shortly after they had grown in. His filthy clothes clung to him in rags.

Herman's passion, his one redeeming quality, was his ability to hunt. His stealth and cunning in the forest were unequaled by his friends or even the men of the village. When he went into the woods, he didn't carry a rifle or a bow. He simply strapped to his legs a pair of knives—throwing daggers—which he could flick silently and with lethal accuracy.

Moving quietly through the forest, he would spot a rabbit or a deer. Before the hapless animal was aware of his presence, a blade would be stuck deep in its heart, blood flowing freely from the mortal wound. A vicious, self-satisfied sneer would curl on the lips of its snaggletoothed killer.

Herman LeRoux managed to grow from infancy to adulthood practically unnoticed by anyone other than his two neighboring companions, Buck Meesley and Sam Moilanen.

———

Born the day after Herman, in the very next shanty, was Sam Moilanen, the first son of Bjorn and Olga. His Finnish-Swedish family had roots in the U.P. going back as far as anyone could remember.

Sam Moilanen, even as a boy, was tall and gangly. His broad Scandinavian forehead belied his mediocre intelligence. From the time Sam first gazed across the vast Great Lakes horizon, he wanted to be on the water. He didn't care whether it was to wade in the shallows of Little Perch Bay on hot July days or to fish with his father and uncles aboard the family fishing boat—a trawler they were destined to lose during the lean years of the fishing famine.

Sam's aunts and uncles, desolate and desperate, slowly drifted away from Little Perch Bay and northern Michigan, which they had once called "God's Country." They migrated south to the foundries and factories of Detroit, Cleveland and Chicago.

Sam's dad and mom, Bjorn and Olga, along with their children, stayed behind in Little Perch Bay. Bjorn was sure the fish would soon return and he could earn enough money to buy another boat.

Bjorn worked for pennies—beers, actually—and was grateful for that. Finally, when Sam was eleven, his mother could take the shame no longer. She walked to Rosa's Market in the center of Little Perch Bay and made a collect call to her brother in Detroit. She asked him to come and take them all away. Bjorn flew into a rage. He would not hear of it. If she wanted to go, fine. But when the fish returned and he got his new boat, she'd best not come crawling back to him.

Immediately after, Bjorn began to fill Sam's head with how it was going to be—how rich they would become. Two weeks later when Sam's uncle came with his truck to take them south, Sam ran into the woods and hid until his mom and his uncle had left for the Lower Peninsula. Bjorn and Sam were on their own.

From then on, Sam was often called upon to help his father home on nights when the seas were especially rough—as they can become when a man spends an entire afternoon and evening at Finney's Bar. Bjorn's job of mending other fishermen's nets didn't pay enough to include food for Sam. And, as the fish became fewer, the nets lasted longer. Bjorn began washing dishes at Finney's to pay for his beer. He often slept in a booth after the bar closed.

By the time Sam was fifteen he was staying at Buck's shanty to avoid the beatings that Bjorn would give him after stumbling home drunk.

The third boy born that week in the next squalid shack was Seamus Meesley, known almost immediately as "Buck" for his fiery disposition. His father, Liam, was a brutish, broad-shouldered, rogue of a man. A thick curly mat of orangy-red hair covered Liam's entire body, giving him the appearance of an unkempt Irish setter. Buck's parents had emigrated from Kinsale, County Cork, when the market for mackerel along the south coast of Ireland fell into decline. In desperation, Liam sold his house and fishing trawler and bought two one-way, steerage-class tickets to America. He came to the rich fishing grounds of northern Michigan. With the remainder of his money he bought a boat, which he named the *Irish Eyes* and a small cabin on the edge of the village. Not long after that, the once profitable northern Michigan fishing industry began to fail.

Buck had seven older siblings who, in such a harsh environment, slowly eroded his mother and father's once strict parenting instincts. By the time Buck was five years old, he was pretty much on his own. Little was done to control his mean-spirited activities. He was free to come and go as he pleased.

Buck, true to his name, loved to fight. He went to school it seemed, simply to bully classmates into a match. The brawls after the last bell always resulted in victory for Buck—bloody and bruised, but invariably less so than his opponents.

He spared his neighbors, Sam and Herman, from daily punishments merely to have accomplices for his other hooligan activities. Besides, he knew they were no match for him. He could knock them down any time he wanted. It was no bother to Buck—so he seldom bothered.

Buck did all the talking for his pals, too. By the time they started school, Sam and Herman had no say in

40

any matter. But that was all right with them, because Buck protected them from the older boys. Of the three, Buck Meesley was the uncontested master. His two subordinates did what he said, where he said and when he said to do it.

If Buck had a fancy to skip school, he had a pair of willing truants who would gladly tag along. When Buck wanted to knock out the town's one streetlight, he had two able watchmen at hand while he pegged baseball-sized rocks at the glowing target until once again, Little Perch Bay was cast into darkness.

Life was hard all year long in Little Perch Bay, but it was especially so in the winters. Temperatures dipped below zero for weeks on end while snow built up, bringing all activities, except school, to a halt. Walking and driving within the village was difficult, but travel between towns was impossible.

One brutally cold February day when Buck was twelve, his mother fell ill. She screamed in pain throughout the night. The following morning Buck walked with his dad five miles through two feet of new snow into De Tour Village to fetch the only doctor in that whole part of the eastern U.P. When they reached the office, ol' Doc Grimson took one look outside and shook his head. He'd never make it through that kind of snow, he said. Instead he sent Buck's dad home with some pills to stop the pain.

That night, Buck's mother got worse. Buck went to sleep with globs of soft candle wax in his ears to muffle her tortured cries. The next morning Buck woke up to find his father sitting on the other side of the one-room shack, his head slumped in his hands. Buck walked over to see what was wrong. He stared at his parents' bed and into his mother's lifeless grey eyes. She was dead.

Seamus "Buck" Measley silently swore he would

41

get back at the doctor who wouldn't come. That very day he met with his two pals, Herman and Sam and made a plan.

A week later, an hour after sundown, three twelve-year-old boys set off through a blinding snowstorm to the neighboring town five miles away. A white frame house in De Tour Village burned to the ground that night. Its sole inhabitant, Doctor Grimson, was trapped upstairs. He died in the blaze, burned to an unrecognizable crisp.

The boys covered their trail out of town and trudged back through the driving snow. They were frozen to the bone and almost dead themselves by the time they sneaked back inside their wretched shanties.

The secret of the tragic fire was never discovered. The unspoken vow as to the unspeakable deed would be locked like a rat in a trap in the minds of three twelve-year-old boys forever.

————

Buck's one ray of light was that he was a great help to his father on the fishing boat. When Buck was fourteen and nearing the end of eighth grade, he suddenly dropped out of school. His departure came as no surprise to anyone and was, in fact, silently cheered by classmates and teachers alike. He joined his father on the trawler, where he worked as a deck hand, tirelessly setting the nets and hauling them in.

Two years later his dad caught pneumonia after a November storm. Liam Meesley died on Christmas Eve. Buck's present that year was the inheritance of the *Irish Eyes*—and all the work and responsibility that went with it. He was sixteen years old and man enough to handle it.

Channel Marker-Red Nun

CHAPTER 8
NEW COURSE

The November gale was getting worse. The stinging rain was turning to shards of ice and penetrating the faces and hands of the fishermen aboard the *Irish Eyes*. After the nets had been stowed away and Sam and Herman had gone below to their hammocks, Buck set his course for Little Perch Bay.

He knew that something had to be done. The fishing hopes were over. Years of drudgery and hard work had left nothing but failure and the certainty of losing the *Irish Eyes* to the local banker. Buck's father had slaved to keep it and after his death, Buck had tried to carry on the tradition. Fishing was all he knew. *This is MINE*, Buck thought as he slammed his fist to the wheel. *No sniveling banker is gonna take it from me.*

Buck stared into the relentless gale. Snow and sleet pelted the windscreen as he held his course from the fishing grounds to Little Perch Bay. *I gotta do somethin'! I can't go back!*

Without another thought Buck timed the next wave

and spun the wheel hard to port. The *Irish Eyes* caught the powerful breaker three-quarters on the bow. A wall of water poured over the starboard deck. She went into the trough and Buck strained to keep her in line for the next one.

When it came it crashed amidship, sending the outmatched boat on her side. She took on water and looked to be heading for the bottom of Lake Huron, but somehow her hatches held. With the air trapped in her cabin, the *Irish Eyes*, like some water-soaked mutt, shook herself and popped back to the surface. Buck muscled the rudder and the next monstrous whitecap washed over the deck at three-quarters astern. A flood of green wash crashed over the rail and drained from the scuppers. Buck strained to keep the wheel hard over. He looked to the next wave. It came directly from the stern.

He had done it! He had come about! Now, there would be no turning back.

The compass at his side responded slowly, but when it settled, it read south-by-southwest toward Cheboygan—a direction and destination, which was in every way, exactly opposite that of Little Perch Bay. Now, a flood of ideas poured into Buck's head.

Three hours later Buck yelled down to his sleeping crew. "Get up here!"

Buck's call roused Sam and Herman from their fitful slumbers. They scrambled to the bridge and stood alongside their captain, intently searching the horizon for buoys or landmarks. Buck pointed into the distance at a tiny dot, which only a seasoned sailor could tell was anything other than a speck of driftwood on the rolling seas. It alternately appeared and disappeared as the *Irish Eyes* crested each wave and then settled into its following trough. "We're not far now."

Buck kept the bobbing can in sight for several

minutes before making his announcement. "He ain't gonna like this," he said casually to Sam and Herman as the *Irish Eyes* passed a red buoy off to her starboard.

"Who ain't gonna like what?" Herman asked. Herman was feeling better already, even though the boat was still rising and falling in the long swells.

"That banker ain't gonna like it that we don't show up in Little Perch Bay," Buck said.

Sam checked the red nun they had just passed. It read 21—not 57, as did the marker at the entrance of their home port! "Where are we?" he asked with a puzzled look.

"Cheboygan," Buck answered nonchalantly.

"Cheboygan?" Herman said. "What're we doin' there?"

"Makin' a career change, eh?" Buck said. "I been doin' some thinkin'. I got it all figgered out so's we kin make a pile a money—an' never haf t' work again."

The <u>Town Crier</u> Office

CHAPTER 9
A LEAD

Pete and his friends finished their lunch at the Andersons' cottage and walked from the back door toward the barn.

"Uncle George didn't appear upset that we took his dinghy out of the harbor," Dan said as he led the way.

"And Aunt Nancy just seemed glad that we were interested in Round Island's history," Kate added.

"Well, we *did* skip the part about getting caught in the current," Eddie said.

Pete pulled the barn door open. "I noticed that nobody told them about the note in the dinghy," he added. "And we didn't exactly *drop* those plates."

"I didn't say *we* did," Kate defended. "I said, *the plates were dropped.*"

Pete shook his head. "When I grow up, I hope I have a way with words like you do. I'll bet there's good money in it somewhere."

Kate pushed her bike out of the barn. "Let's hurry," she said. "Ginny told us to meet her at the <u>Town Crier</u> by one o'clock. It's a quarter 'til right now."

47

"Hi, Ginny," Kate said as she led the others into the one-room office. She glanced around and saw that no one else was there. "How's the newspaper biz?"

"Hi, Kate." The slim, dark-haired, fifteen-year-old flashed a welcoming smile. "Frantic. It's summer. Need I say more? How's it going, Dan?—Eddie? Who's your friend?"

"This is Pete Jenkins," Kate answered. "He's our neighbor in the Snows."

"What's up?" Ginny asked, turning to Kate. "I know you too well to think that this is just a social visit."

"Yes, well, something *has* sort of cropped up," Kate replied. "All right, Ginny, I'll get right to it. Have you heard any talk about Round Island lately?"

"You mean like someone building cottages on it?" Ginny said. "It's been off-limits to anything like that since it became part of the state park. Now all it does is sit in the water and look pretty. In fact, no one is even allowed there—except Indians. Even *they* don't go very often. College kids—you know, summer workers here on Mackinac—they might have a cookout once in a while, but other than that . . . " She shook her head and went back to stacking a bale of newspapers on a delivery cart.

"How about the lighthouse keeper, Jesse Muldoon?" Pete asked. "Have you heard anything about him?"

"Funny you should mention him," Ginny said, straightening up and looking into the distance. "Last week I heard someone tell my dad that he saw a man walking along the shore over there. It was the dead of night—way before dawn. The man was shrouded in darkness, silhouetted in the moonlight. He moved like a ghost in the mist. Very eerie." She paused and then stared at her visitors in turn as if drawing bits of information from their

48

eyes. "All right, out with it. You guys are up to something. What's going on?"

As Kate explained what had happened on Round Island, Ginny's interest grew. She nodded as Kate finished her curious account. "I hadn't thought much about it," Ginny said, "but a number of things, unrelated until what you just told me, now fall into place. As for Jesse Muldoon, I don't know where he is. He *could* be on Round. He could be here on Mackinac—so much of it is state park wilderness. There are hundreds of places to stay—old barns, caves, abandoned cabins. For all I know he might have moved away or even died. But his name does pop up every now and then. People have seen some*one* or some*thing* over there near the lighthouse late at night."

"And they think it might be Mr. Muldoon?" Kate asked.

"They won't swear to it, but they say it *could* be him—him or his ghost. Whether Jesse had anything to do with what happened to you this morning, I don't know."

"If not Mr. Muldoon, who might have left that message?" Kate asked.

Ginny walked to the door and glanced outside. She searched in all directions before returning to her visitors. "There *is* someone else," she whispered. "He's kind of a vagrant—a bum, really. His name is Herman LeRoux. He's been on the Island all summer. He started as a dishwasher at the Windsor but got canned—stole some stuff from the kitchen. Instead of leaving Mackinac, he started hanging around town, sleeping in barns and on park benches. Suddenly, he began to flash money—lots of it. He'd go to the Mustang or Liquor Horn's and buy rounds. People would ask him where he was working—you know, like they were glad for him that he had found a job. He'd just smile and say that he had come into some money. Well, that was a little hard to believe. He had no address where someone could send him this windfall. I figured he had to be stealing it."

"What could this Herman-guy have to do with what happened to us on Round Island?" Dan asked.

"I'm getting to that," Ginny said. "I wouldn't have thought about him except last week a man told my dad that he saw Herman at about 3 A.M rowing toward the old lighthouse. The waves were too rough for anyone to be out there just for some fresh air. Word got around town pretty fast and most people figured Herman was finally leaving the Island. Good riddance, too. But a few days later he showed up here again. He must have come back during the night or someone would have seen him rowing and told my dad. Whatever mischief he's up to, he's doing it in the wee hours of the night."

"Where can we find him?" Dan asked.

"Depends on if he's come into some more money or not," Ginny said. "If he has, he'll be at one of the bars. If not, you might find him sleeping under a tree. But if I were you, I wouldn't go looking for him. He had a roommate when he was working for the Windsor, a British fellow—a cook, I think. Anyway, this British guy said he came into his room one night after his shift and found Herman sitting on the floor with the beds and mattresses set on their sides like he was in his own little séance chamber. Tall candles were burning all around him and Herman was sitting cross-legged, holding a dead chicken up by its feet. Blood was dripping from its beak into a Mason jar. Who knows what that's all about?"

Kate caught Dan's eye with a glance, each remembering their dream of the night before with the three men on Round Island sitting as if in a séance around a campfire in the Indian burial ground.

"Have the police been able to find out about him?"

50

Eddie asked. "Maybe he's wanted somewhere."

"He doesn't sound like anyone *I'd* ever want," Pete said.

Ginny flashed a smile at the newcomer. "That's just what I'm trying to impress upon your friends, Pete." She turned to Kate, her manner once again serious. "Herman LeRoux is no one to mess with. If you're half as bright as you think you are, you'll avoid this guy like the Crack-In-The-Island on a dark night. People seem to think Mackinac is nothing more that a resort spot for rich folks. But in truth, it's been a magnet for all sorts of bad guys going back to the 1600s. Until recently, it was on the very edge of the civilized world. If a man wanted to get away from his problems, he'd come here. Then, if someone came looking for him, he could just take that easy step into the uncharted wilderness and be lost to all but the Algonquin people who dwelt in its darkest forests. Even now, this isn't as carefree and happy-go-lucky a place as the Chamber of Commerce would like you to believe—for most people, yes, but not for *all* people."

"So," Kate said, "when did you see him last?"

"Weren't you listening?" Ginny said. "Look, I don't want to be the one who typesets your death notices. Do yourselves a big favor and drop the whole thing. Hey, I've got to run. These papers won't deliver themselves. Please tell me you won't get involved with Herman LeRoux, okay?"

Kate smiled. "How about if we just promise to be careful?"

Ginny shook her head in resignation and pushed her cart out into the clean, bright Straits of Mackinac afternoon.

Wawashkamo Clubhouse

CHAPTER 10
GOLF

"Ginny's right," Eddie said. "Maybe we got lucky over on Round Island with just a few broken plates. I say we forget the whole thing. How about some golf? Do you play golf, Pete?"

"Never have before," Pete said, "but compared with Kate's idea of chasing that Herman guy, it sounds great."

Kate stared, as if in shock, at the three boys. "You're not going to let Ginny Lind's wild tale about some bum keep us from having some fun, are you?" she said. "Ginny's learned from her father how to make everything sound worse than it is. That's what the newspaper business is all about. That's how they sell papers. She even *talks* in headlines. And dramatic?—`The man was shrouded in darkness . . . he moved like a ghost in the mist.' Come on. She's just trying to scare us."

"If scaring people stiff is what she's learning," Pete said, "I'd say she's got that lesson pretty well in her hip pocket."

Dan stepped toward the door. "Eddie and Pete are right," he said. "We're tempting fate for no good reason.

Let's go up to Wawashkamo and play nine holes. Besides, being on the same golf course with Eddie and his boomerang drives should be adventure enough for anyone—even you, Kate."

Kate's disgusted expression fell upon each of them in turn. "All right," she said, "but I think we'll be missing out on some great fun. Where would the Hardy Boys be if every time a crook came along Joe and Frank decided to go golfing?"

"This isn't the Hardy Boys, Kate," Eddie said. "This is for real."

"Well, `for real' can be pretty dull if you don't look for exciting stuff to do," Kate said. "I hope you all drive your tee shots into the woods and get poison ivy." The very thought raised her spirits and made her break out in a good laugh.

"It's settled then," said Dan. "Golf it is. We'll call Aunt and Uncle and tell them we're going up to Wawashkamo."

———

The four pedaled their bikes to the top of the island, taking the British Landing Road to the Wawashkamo Links clubhouse. The classic, wood-framed building with its red shutters and green roof was nestled among huge pine trees that shaded the entire setting. The kids parked their bikes and walked on a thick, spongy blanket of pine needles to the front door. There, Mr. Dennis, the club pro, greeted them.

"Hello, Kate. Hi, Eddie, Dan," he said with a welcoming nod. "Your uncle called and told me to expect you. It's a great day for golf—but then they all are, as far as I'm concerned." He turned to Pete and smiled, handing him a bag of clubs. "And you must be Peter Jenkins. Mr. Anderson says that you might be kind of new at this, so I've put together a special set. I've taken all the hooks and

54

slices out of the woods and irons and given you my special hole-seeking putter. You shouldn't have any trouble at all."

"Gee, thanks, Mr. Dennis," Pete said, looking into the bag.

"There aren't many people on the course right now," Mr. Dennis said to Dan. "The greens are playing a little fast today. It's been dry, you know. Oh and Eddie, I've seen that hook of yours. Some people say your drives are the only reason no large game animals live here on Mackinac. The deer and raccoon are drawn to your tee shots like moths to a lantern. The smart ones left for the mainland when you took up the game."

"Very funny," Eddie said, "but it's not all *that* bad."

"Really though," Mr. Dennis said seriously, "try not to hook one into the woods on number seven. Rumor has it that a hobo is hanging around the old Early barn—maybe even living there. Folks tell me it's some young, nasty-looking derelict with a short temper. He isn't friendly toward golfers—or anyone else, probably."

Remembering Ginny Lind's description of Herman LeRoux, Dan glanced nervously at his sister. Their eyes locked for a moment and then Dan's gaze swung to Eddie. An uneasy look crossed Eddie's face, too. Pete, meanwhile, was staring at his putter, trying to figure out where the "hole-seeking" thingy was.

"I'll be careful," Eddie said. The four shouldered their golf bags and moved toward the first tee. Once there, Pete watched Dan and Eddie as each stretched his arms, legs and back. He then imitated them as best he could, trying not to look goofy.

"You can go first, Pete," Dan said.

Pete had never actually played on a golf course, but he had gone to a driving range once. He unzipped the pouch on the golf bag and took out a ball. He fished

55

around in the bottom. "There's no tee in here," he said. "Can I borrow one of yours?"

"They don't use regular wooden tees on this course," Dan said. "Here, they set the ball on a little pile of dirt like they do in Scotland. I'll show you." Dan reached into a nearby pail and scooped out a handful of sand. He formed an inch-high mound and set the ball on top. "There you go," he said moving back. "Let 'er rip."

Pete stepped up, took a huge back swing and launched the head of his driver in the general direction of the small, white sphere.

Swoooosh.

But no *ping*. The ball remained atop its earthen perch.

"You peeked," Eddie said.

"Huh?" Pete said, blood rushing to his cheeks in embarrassment.

"You raised your head," Eddie explained. "You've got to keep your head down. Other than that, it was perfect. Try again."

Pete walked away and took a practice stroke, this time aiming at the fuzzy head of an old dandelion. *Swoosh*. The flower exploded into a cloud of airborne seeds, raising Pete's confidence. He returned to the tee. Again, the big back swing and *Swoosh*.

Clunk.

The club topped the ball and sent it dribbling into the fairway about thirty yards. Pete glowered as it trickled to a halt.

He turned to Kate. "Can we go home yet?" he asked, his face now hot and fully flushed.

"No, your swing was great, Pete," Kate said with a snicker. "You just need a little more distance. Maybe if you would actually *hit* the ball rather than expecting it to move entirely by wind pressure—that might help."

56

"No, no, no," Dan said, barely stifling a laugh. "Don't listen to Kate. The way you do it you'll never lose a ball. See? It's right out there. No, don't change a thing, Pete. That's the problem with a lot of golfers. They hit it too far and then they can't find it."

"It's a good thing Mr. Dennis took the hook and the slice out of your club," Eddie continued. "The ball might have ended up twenty yards to the left or right. Then where would you be?"

Pete stared at his three friends. "You know," he said, "I heard that Bobby Jones, the greatest golfer of all time, once wrapped a nine-iron around the neck of a guy who made a wisecrack in the gallery."

"I might be worried if I thought you could hit me," Eddie chortled.

"That does it. I'm going home. You can just play with your little piles of sand without me." Pete shoved his driver into the bag and turned for the clubhouse.

"Aw, come on Pete," Kate said, putting her arm around his waist. "We were just teasing. That's part of the game. If it weren't for golf, people would go around thinking they were perfect. Look, let's be partners. Dan and Eddie against you and me. We'll kill them."

"Really?" Pete said with a smirk. "You mean if we win, we can *kill* them? I'm all for *that*." Besides, being partners with Kate in anything was an offer Pete could never refuse.

———

By the end of six holes, the score was even. Dan was a little wild with his drives, but Eddie on each of his tee shots, hooked his ball about a mile out of bounds. Kate was an unbelievably good golfer. Her woods and irons were always straighter if not longer than Dan's and Eddie's. And Pete *did* seem to have a hole-seeking putter. He had sunk five of his team's six putts. The four stood together at the seventh tee, looking out at the fairway.

"It's a straight, four-hundred-yard par four," Dan said. "Eddie, the Early barn is off to the left behind those trees—or need I remind you?"

"No, I've been thinking about it for six holes now," Eddie said. He reached into the pail for a handful of sand. He set his ball on the pile and stepped back. He took two practice swings, moved up to the ball and whacked it. It shot beautifully, straight down the fairway, still climbing as it passed the 150-yard mark. Then, just as with his previous six drives, the ball began a slow, graceful curve to the left. By about the 200-yard mark it was traveling sideways across the fairway. It drifted out of bounds over the top of a dense forest of cedars.

Thud!

It was not the sound of a ball hitting a tree. It sounded more as if it had struck a building—perhaps a barn.

"I believe you will find it somewhere in the vicinity of Mr. Early's cowshed," Dan said.

"No, I don't think so," Eddie said slowly. "I believe that ball is gone forever. I, for one, have no intention of looking for it. We'll play your shot this time, Dan. Tee it up and hit it straight. I don't care how far, just straight."

Dan stepped to the tee. He set his feet, looked down the fairway and let fly. His ball screamed off the tee—a great drive—*if he'd lined it up properly*. Instead, it went straight for the left rough.

"Oh, no!" he yelled as it arched over the same trees that Eddie's had.

Thud!

It was the very sound that had marked the end of Eddie's shot.

"I don't suppose you would mind if we gave you

this hole, would you?" Eddie asked Kate.

"Not so fast," she said. "We'll help you look for the balls. Besides, I want to see that barn."

After Pete's fifty-yard dribbler, Kate teed up and smacked her drive 180 yards down the middle. Pete picked up his ball and the four headed toward the rough.

Herman's Hideout

CHAPTER 11
THIEF'S NEST

The four golfers spread out along the out-of-
bounds line where each thought the stray drives had gone
into the woods. Pete went in through some low-lying
cedar shrubs. He poked his head into the clearing and
there, sixty feet away, a weather-beaten barn stood.

"Over here!" Pete called out.

"Pete!" Kate screamed. "Are you okay? Dan!
Eddie! Come quick!" In no time all three were huddled
around Pete.

"What's wrong?" Pete said, glancing from one
worried face to another.

"You're not hurt?" Dan asked.

"No," Pete said. "Why would I be?"

"We thought you were getting beaten up by that
guy Mr. Dennis told us about."

"What guy?" Pete said, blinking in surprise. "I just
called you over to show you this barn. That's what Kate
wanted to see, right?—where Dan's and Eddie's drives
landed? I bet there was a farm around here once. Imagine
that—a farm right here on Mackinac Island!"

"Don't scare us like that," Kate said. "We thought you were getting killed or something."

"Well, if it was so dangerous, why didn't you warn me?"

"We figured you knew," said Dan. "Didn't you hear Mr. Dennis tell about the bum who has been bothering golfers lately? We were afraid it might be Herman What's-His-Name that Ginny Lind told us about—the guy who broke up our picnic on Round Island."

"I must have missed that part," Pete said.

"Well, he's evidently not here or he'd be screaming at us by now," Eddie said. "I say we forget the lost balls and get back on the course."

"Wait a minute," Kate said. "Let's search that barn. If it *is* the same guy that broke up our picnic this morning, then he's still on Round Island. Remember? Ginny said he must be traveling by night or someone would have seen him rowing during the day."

"That's right," said Dan. "Maybe something in the barn will tell us what he's doing over there."

"What if it's not the same guy?" Pete said. "What if the man Mr. Dennis was talking about is still in the barn sound asleep?"

"I doubt, with two direct hits on his bedroom wall, he'd be resting too comfortably," Kate said. "From inside, those balls must have sounded like cannon shots. Whoever it is, by now, he'd be out here, giving us an earful."

"We're wasting time," Dan said. "My bet is that the guy who's staying here *is* Herman and he's on Round Island right now. I'm with Kate. Let's see what's in there." He turned toward the open door. Kate was right with him. Pete glanced at Eddie, who shrugged and followed Dan and Kate into the barn.

Although there were no windows, plenty of light filtered through the cracks and missing boards of the musty building. It was not a large barn, about the size of a two-car garage—more like a storage shed.

"Well, I don't see anything," Pete said, turning quickly for the exit. "Let's go."

"Wait," Kate said. "There's a ladder going up to the loft."

"The rungs don't look very sturdy," Eddie said. "I wouldn't trust it."

"Looks strong enough for me," said Kate. Without hesitation, she scaled the ladder to the upper floor.

"Guys! Come here!" she yelled. "Hurry!"

Dan was on his way. Eddie tested the first step with all his weight—then the second—then joined the others in the stifling heat of the poorly ventilated loft. Pete waited for Eddie to clear the top rung and then slowly followed. What they found would have made a mother cringe. A bale of straw had been used as a makeshift bed. A pair of grimy overalls and a few tattered shirts were tossed in a corner. Bread wrappers and tin cans littered the area. Apparently, the man had no one around to tell him to clean his room.

"Okay, so?" Eddie said, turning to Kate. "The guy's a slob. It doesn't make him a criminal."

"This might," Kate said, uncovering a faded green metal container about the size of Pete's tackle box.

"What do you suppose is in it?" Dan whispered.

Kate fumbled with the latch. "It's kind of rusty. I can't open it."

"Let me try," Dan said. He took the box and moved over by the wall where a missing board let in a beam of dusty sunlight.

"Hurry," Pete said, peering through a knothole. "The guy could come in here any second."

"There, I've got it," Dan said. The hinged top creaked and Dan peered inside. He glanced first at a hand-drawn map of Mackinac Island with X's and O's along the East and West Bluffs. He put that back and took out a thin packet.

"Open it," Kate urged.

Dan carefully loosened the tape, revealing a wad of money. He fanned the bills for the others to see. "Looks like about a thousand dollars," he said. He resealed the envelope and reached deeper into the box, where he found a thick booklet.

"It's this year's Great Lakes shipping schedule," Dan said. He began turning the pages until he came to a section heavily smudged with use. "This part lists every boat that comes through northern Lake Huron, with the scheduled date and time of its passing various lighthouses."

"You're kidding," Eddie said. "What would a bum want with that?"

"I don't know," Dan said, "but two names are underlined: here on this page, the *V.A. Frazier* and over here on this page, the *Quince*. Look here. Today, August 20th at 03:30, the *V.A. Frazier* passed through between Mackinac and Round Island."

"03:30," Eddie said. "That's military talk for 3:30 A.M! Do you think that's what Herman's been doing in the middle of the night?—going out and meeting freighters?"

"No freighters stop at Round Island," Kate said. "There's no dock. And I've never seen a freighter dead in the water anywhere around here except waiting to be locked through at the Sault."

"I don't get it, either," Dan said, "but the next underlined entry is for the *Quince* on August 23rd. It doesn't say what time it comes through, but those are the

64

only two ships that are underlined in the whole book."

"That looks like an official government publication," Kate said. "How would a shiftless bum have gotten such a thing?"

"Maybe he stole it from the Coast Guard station in town," Eddie said.

"Or maybe it was given to him by a certain lighthouse keeper," Pete added. "Like Jesse Muldoon. Holy cow! Maybe it's Mr. Muldoon who's staying here."

"Nah," Eddie said. "Jesse Muldoon must be in his eighties. Besides, Mr. Dennis told us it was a young guy staying here."

"There's something very strange about all of this," Kate murmured.

"Let's get out of here," said Pete. "Whoever's staying in this barn probably doesn't like it when golf balls bounce off his bedroom wall, but I bet he really hates it when people mess with his stash box."

"I'm with Pete," Eddie said. "Let's turn in our clubs."

"We're not going to finish the match?" Kate asked in amazement.

"Let's just call it a tie," Eddie said.

"`Tie' nothing," Kate contested. "You'll going to admit defeat, or we'll play it out."

"Okay, you win," Dan said as he closed the lid on the green container. "I've had enough golf for one day. Where did you find this, Kate?"

"In the corner under some straw. Here, I'll put it back."

The three boys watched as Kate returned the box to its hiding place, then slid down the ladder, gathered their golf bags and hurried back to the seventh fairway.

The *V.A. Frazier*

CHAPTER 12
THE MYSTERY SHIPS

After coming out of the woods, the four stood together on the edge of the rough. "I don't think we should tell Mr. Dennis about this," Kate said.

"Right," Dan agreed. "Until we find out more, let's keep quiet about the whole thing."

"If it was up to me," Pete said, "I'd tell the police and be done with it. But I'll guess for you three that would be out of the question."

"That's right," Kate responded. "Totally. Besides, there *are* no police. Remember? The one Mackinac policeman, Chief Chamberlain, is in jail."

"I can't believe they haven't replaced him yet," Eddie said.

"Well, they haven't," said Dan. "So until they do, I guess we'll have to be the keepers of justice for Mackinac Island all by ourselves."

"I like that, `The Keepers of Justice,'" Kate said.

"Sounds too much like some Wild West vigilantes," Pete said.

"Besides," said Kate, ignoring Pete's observation,

"what would we tell the police anyway?—that we went inside an old barn and found some money?—and a load of trash? I'd say my fellow detectives, we don't really have much on this guy."

"So, what are we going to do?" Pete asked.

"Well, we've got three days until the *Quince* comes through," Dan said. "Let's keep our eyes on the barn, the lighthouse and Herman."

"How are we going to do all that?" Pete asked. "We can't hang around here day and night until he shows up."

"No, but we could set a twig in front of his barn door," Kate suggested. "We could check it every day—maybe pretend we're playing golf—and when we see that the stick has been moved, we know he's been back."

"Then we could go to his loft," Dan said, "look inside the green box and find out what he got when he met with the freighter."

"What if, when we get upstairs, he's still sleeping? Or worse yet, that he's just waking up?" Pete asked. "It's not as if we can just go knock on his door like we're three Avon Ladies."

"Great idea," Kate said. "That's just what we'll do."

"I meant that as a joke," Pete said. "He probably has all the aftershave and soap-on-a-rope he'll ever want. And, as the sales guy, I wouldn't want to tell him he could stand a little freshening up."

"No, I mean we can knock on his door," said Kate eagerly. "Eddie, what are your chances of landing another drive against that barn?"

"Pretty good, I'm afraid," Eddie said. "I'd have a lot harder time hitting the ball straight."

"Then that's the ticket," Kate said. "Pete, you have the best ideas! Come on, let's set a twig in his doorway.

Tomorrow we'll go golfing and Eddie will knock another ball against the barn. If someone doesn't start screaming at us, we'll check out the stick. If it's been moved, we'll know he's been back and has left again. We'll go up to the loft and check out the box. Easy as pie."

"In the meantime," Dan said, "we could go to the Coast Guard station and find out about the *Quince* and the *V.A. Frazier*. Then maybe we could nose around town and learn more about Herman."

"I bet his old roommate, the cook at the Windsor, could tell us something," Eddie said.

———

"That was quick," Mr. Dennis said as the four carried their bags in from the course. "Any problems with our friend on seven?"

"Nope, he wasn't around," Dan said. "But we were wondering what he looks like. Have you ever seen him?"

"No," the golf pro said. "But several people have told me he's in his early twenties. He has long, black hair and no front teeth. He's short, but muscular—and real rough looking. I doubt you would mistake him for a college professor. If you ever see him on the course, take my advice. Turn and walk away."

"Thanks," Dan said. "We'll be back tomorrow."

The four jumped on their bikes and headed toward town. The ride, downhill all the way, was much faster than on the way up. In minutes they were standing before a uniformed man at the Coast Guard station.

"Excuse me, sir," Dan said, "we're looking for some information about two boats."

"What kind of boats?" the Coast Guardsman said.

"Freighters," Dan answered. "Do you have a roster of Great Lakes ships?"

"Right here," the man said. "Which two did you have in mind?"

69

"The *V.A. Frazier* and the *Quince*," said Kate.

The man fidgeted for a moment and then asked, "Why do you want to know?"

"We're helping Ginny Lind at the <u>Town Crier</u>," said Dan. "She's doing a story on Great Lakes shipping for her weekly column."

The man nodded and opened his book. "Here we are," he said, "the *Virginia Ann Frazier*. She's a 500-foot, Tartan Steel carrier out of Chicago. Her captain is Melvin Edwards, who operates with a crew of eighteen. It came through, light, this morning at 03:30, logged in by Officer Timkins. What was the name of the other ship?"

"The *Quince*," Dan said.

"Hmm, that doesn't sound familiar," the man said, flipping the pages. "It's not under `Q.' Are you sure it's a freighter?"

Kate looked surprised. "Well, no, not really," she said.

"I'll check the other register," the Coast Guard officer said, reaching behind him for a thinner publication. "We don't monitor these as carefully. Here, maybe this is it: The *Quince*— built in Algonac, Michigan, in 1883. She's a seventy-foot, two-masted schooner, sailing out of Cheboygan now and making the North Channel her only port of call. She was once a lumber carrier but was dry-docked in 1925 and has been out of service until last year. This past November she was bought and refitted by a new owner, Buck Meesley. It's listed currently as a charter pleasure craft."

"So she just goes back and forth between Cheboygan and the North Channel without an exact timetable?" Dan asked.

"That's correct, but since Mr. Meesley sails for profit, he has to license her as a commercial vessel and file a statement of her approximate schedule."

70

"So, if the *Quince* comes past here, for example, she doesn't have to report in like the freighters do?" Kate asked.

"Right again," the officer said.

"Thank you, sir," Kate said. "Let's go, guys."

The four friends went outside to the bicycle rack in the warm breeze of Biddle Point.

"Where to now?" Eddie said.

"The Windsor Hotel," Dan answered, hopping on his bike.

The Windsor Hotel

CHAPTER 13
LEONARD COLESMITH

Dan Hinken walked alone into the dimly-lit lobby of the Windsor Hotel on Market Street. The place was like a museum, having changed little since the day it opened in 1890. Dark paneled walls and formal Victorian furniture were daunting to all but its wealthy, seventy-and-up clientele.

"Excuse me, ma'am," Dan said after waiting for several moments at the registry window. He tapped the wooden placard that read, Miss Agnes Talley, Proprietress.

A minute passed. When it became evident that the young man would not go away, the grey-haired woman looked up from her desk with an exasperated sniff, "May I be of service?"

"My uncle asked me to help him find his son, my cousin," Dan said. "The last we heard, he was working here at the Windsor."

"And who might this fellow be?" Miss Talley asked.

"His name is Herman LeRoux," Dan answered.

"He's twenty-one years old, five-foot-six, dark hair, muscular, . . . "

"I am familiar with Mr. LeRoux's description," Miss Talley interrupted, eyeing skeptically her fair-skinned visitor. "He was our dishwasher. He assumed the position held for thirty years by Mr. Beresford, who passed away last winter. Your *cousin*, however, is no longer in our employ. I regret to say that Herman was neither as capable in his duties nor as trustworthy in his character as his predecessor. Since his dismissal, I have neither seen him, nor do I wish to."

"It's important that I find him," Dan said. "His mother is very sick—not expected to live. She has asked us to bring him home. Would any of your staff know where he might be?"

Miss Tally stared dubiously at her young visitor, but then shrugged and said, "While employed, Herman roomed with Mr. Colesmith. He's been our chef these past forty years. You may speak with Leonard, but I doubt he will be of much help. The two had little in common. Follow me. Mr. Colesmith will be in the kitchen just now, preparing the evening meal. Do be brief."

Dan followed Miss Talley along a dark hallway and through a small, dimly-lit dining area where a white-haired woman was setting tables. Another narrow hallway ended at a swinging door, which Miss Talley pushed open. Dan followed her into a cold, clammy kitchen, with walls and floor of solid, grey stone. A single bare bulb hung ten feet above the room's center. The only other light filtered through an opaque, wave-paned window that looked out onto a weed-choked alley.

Bent over a butcher-block table was a gaunt, elderly man wearing white pants, a tall white hat and a wide, white apron. The entire outfit was deeply stained with blood, grease and other animal materials. His face pale and pasty, he had the unmistakable pallor of someone long removed from even the briefest benefits of sunlight and fresh air. A drop of moisture clung to the tip of his nose and was discharged to the floor as he turned to face his visitors. He, like his clothing, appeared diseased and quite possibly infectious.

Mr. Colesmith held a butcher knife in one hand and a long, limp tenderloin of pork in the other. He gazed uneasily upon his employer and youthful visitor as they entered.

"Leonard, this young man claims to be the cousin of Herman LeRoux," Miss Talley said. "He requests a *very* few minutes of your time. You will be so good as to answer his questions. Now if you will excuse me; I have business to attend to at my desk." She turned on her heel and a moment later the door swung shut behind Miss Talley.

"I am trying to find Herman," Dan said. "Miss Talley tells me that you shared a room. Can you tell me anything about him?—who he might know?—where he might be?"

The man grimaced and shook his head, discharging another droplet from the tip of his nose. His face clouded as though an unpleasant thought had just entered his head.

"Oh, 'e's a bad 'un, 'e is," Mr. Colesmith whispered slowly. He spoke in short, clipped syllables with a thick, almost unintelligible Cockney accent. "I could tell a tale or two, I could. I don't suppose you'd be interested in that, now would you, sir?"

"Yes, I would," Dan said, "especially if it leads me to him."

"Well, I don't know 'ow much this will 'elp, but more than once I came from the kitchen up to my room—I call it *my* room, it's not *mine*, really. I've just stayed there the last forty-some years—shared it with the old

75

dishwasher, Clive Beresford, I did—decent old chap—'e died of consumption this past winter. 'ow he ever caught that, I'll never know. Anyway, I'd come into my room and there Mr. LeRoux would be, standing at one end and throwing daggers into the wall at the other. 'e must 'ave 'ad a 'alf-dozen of 'em. Why 'e 'ad so many was beyond me, but 'e placed a great deal of importance on the accuracy of 'is throws, 'e did—sharpening and cleaning 'em, as well. Oh, 'e would spend hours at that, 'e would."

"Cleaning them?" Dan asked.

"Yes, sir, cleaning 'em," Mr. Colesmith said. "Near as I could tell, those daggers was the only thing 'e 'ad such a fancy for. 'e was, in truth, a filthy young pup. I asked 'im once, I said, `Why do you keep those knives so sharp?' and 'e said, `Sharp blades kill.' That's jus' wha' 'e said. I don't know wha' 'e'd kill on this 'ere island, there being no game whatsoever."

"Did he have any friends?" Dan asked. "Anyone he might have talked to?"

Mr. Colesmith shook his head, sucked in some air and formed the word "no" on his lips. But then he slowly lifted his eyes and met Dan's gaze. "There was this one bloke," the chef said. "Again, I was comin' up to me room when I 'eard loud, angry talk from be'ind the door. I stood there, not wantin' to barge in on some private chit-chat, but just then I 'eard Mr. LeRoux choke out, `No, Buck. I'll do whatever you say.' And then I 'eard another, low-pitched, gravelly voice say, `You better, 'erman, or it'll be the end of you.' As much as I didn't care for Mr. LeRoux, I 'ad to feel sorry for 'im—the fix 'e was in with this Buck fellow."

"What happened then?" Dan asked.

"I went down the stairs, I did and waited till I 'eard the door slam. Then I started up. As the man approached I glanced into 'is face, like you do when you meet someone on a street or a stairway and I got a good look at

76

'im. 'e was a brawny young man, curly red hair and parched, suntanned skin. 'e had on a tight, short-sleeved jersey, no socks and those leather shoes what sailors seem to wear. 'e looked the type you wouldn't dare cross, so whatever business this Mr. Buck 'ad with Mr. LeRoux, I'd say Mr. LeRoux was duty bound to carry it out."

"How long ago was that?" Dan asked.

"Oh, I should say ten days to a fortnight before Miss Talley let Mr. LeRoux go." Yet another drop of clear moisture fell from the chef's nose, contributing to the fair-sized puddle at his feet.

"And how did that happen?"

"Miss Talley tol' me she was missing certain pieces of the 'otel's equipment and asked me to be on the lookout for 'em. I think she suspected 'erman right from the start, so when I found two kitchen knives under 'is bed, I told 'er. After the dinner dishes was done that night, 'erman was gone. That's the last I seen of 'im."

"Thanks, Mr. Colesmith," Dan said. "You've been a big help." Dan pushed open the kitchen door and the chef turned back to his butcher knife and loin of pork.

Mackinac Lighthouse Station

CHAPTER 14
MORE CLUES

"Bingo," Dan said as he approached his three friends. Pete, Eddie and Kate held their bicycles in a half-circle across the street from the Windsor Hotel waiting for his return.

"Would you like to expand on that?" Eddie said casually.

"First of all, Kate was right," Dan began. "It was a good thing we didn't all go together. The lady who owns the place would have run us out in two seconds. As it was, I'm not sure she believed I was Herman's cousin."

"You told her *that?*" Eddie said. "No wonder she didn't believe you."

"I had to tell her something," Dan said, "or she wouldn't have let me talk to the cook."

"Still, that little bit of news hardly rates a `Bingo,'" Eddie said.

Dan grinned. "I'm getting there. So, Miss Talley took me to the kitchen and introduced me to the chef, Leonard Colesmith. The man has a nasty sinus condition. If *he's* not an epidemic waiting to happen, I'm sure his *clothes* are. Anyway, he's Herman's old roommate. Mr.

LeRoux, it seems, is an expert knife thrower—daggers, the cook called them. He practices by the hour and keeps them razor-sharp."

"Scary," Eddie said, "but still not 'Bingo' material."

Dan smiled. "He also works for someone called Buck."

"Wasn't it Buck Meesley who owns the *Quince*?" Pete asked.

"That, my friends, is the 'Bingo'," Dan said calmly. "Buck Meesley, according to the Coast Guard guy. Anyway, Buck came here and gave Herman a hard time. Mr. Colesmith said he didn't know why Buck was so angry but it was clear that Herman had to do something or he would pay for it with his life. So, there's our link between Herman and the *Quince*."

"Swell," Pete said. "Can we butt out now?"

"Why?" Dan asked.

"Haven't you three heard enough?" Pete asked. "The guy we're scared of seeing face to face—a man who plays with knives, fire and for some bizarre reason known only to himself, chicken blood—turns out to be under the thumb of an even scarier guy who might be working for someone else—maybe aboard the *V.A. Frazier*. Whatever their game is, I doubt if it's nearly as much fun as, say, tiddlywinks."

"Oh, come on, Pete," Kate said. "We're not in any danger. We're just kind of watching, you know, from a distance."

"Well, the distance isn't far enough for me," Pete muttered.

"How about we take our minds off it for the rest of the afternoon and just do something really touristy," Eddie said. "We could ride around the island. Maybe stop at British Landing and go out on the old dock."

"That would suit me just fine," Pete said. "If that's

80

as far as we can get from Herman, that's where I want to be."

The four hopped on their bikes and raced along the West Shore Road out of town. In half an hour they coasted up to a decaying stone crib dock that extended thirty feet into the Straits.

"Why is it called British Landing?" Pete asked, setting his kickstand.

"This is where the British troops came ashore in a sneak attack on the Americans in 1812," Dan answered. "The Yankee commander here didn't even know they were at war and the fort was taken without a shot being fired. This could just as well be called `American Landing' because it was also here that our troops tried to return the favor in 1814. It might have worked except the British caught wind of it and were waiting along with their Indian friends at the top of the island where Wawashkamo Golf Course is now. When the Americans crept over the hill, the Redcoats and Indians let 'em have it. Twelve of our guys were killed and by the time the colonel signaled for retreat, only a few were able to get back to the ship. They barely made it off the Island. Tomorrow when we go back to the golf course I'll show you where Major Holmes was killed. It's near the barn where Herman stays."

Pete was standing at the end of the crumbling dock, peering into the transparent depths. "Thanks for reminding me," he muttered.

"Well, you asked," said Dan.

"Since you brought it up," Kate said, "I can't figure out the connection between the *Quince* and the *V.A. Frazier*. One's a modern freighter and the other's an antique charter schooner. How could two such different boats be linked? And what does Mackinac Island have to do with their plan? Neither one is actually supposed to stop here."

81

Back along the shore, Eddie was sitting on a rock holding a stick. His head was bent as he drew in the sand. "What are you doing, Eddie?" Dan asked.

Eddie looked up. "I might be able to answer your question, Kate. Come over here. See what you think."

Dan, Kate and Pete scrambled over the rocks and stood in a circle around Eddie. He had made a sketch of the entire Great Lakes in the sand. "Let's suppose the *V.A. Frazier* carries iron ore," Eddie said.

"That's a fair guess," Kate said. "She's owned by Tartan Steel out of Chicago."

"Right," Eddie said, putting his stick at the southernmost tip of Lake Michigan. He drew a line north to Beaver Island and then east to the Straits. "She goes here between Mackinac and Round Island, past the Snows to De Tour, through the Soo Locks, then west to Duluth where she takes on ore."

"Okay," Kate said, "but what does that have to do with the sailboat?"

Eddie continued, "Well, the skipper of the *Quince*, uh . . ."

"Buck Meesley," Pete put in. "How could you forget a name like that?"

"Yeah, Buck Meesley," Eddie said, "he's out of Cheboygan and takes his passengers up to the North Channel, right?"

"According to the Coast Guard guy," Dan said. "So?"

Eddie put his stick along the northeast shoreline of Michigan's lower peninsula. He drew a line north and east to the North Channel—a route that came nowhere near Mackinac Island nor the course of the *V.A. Frazier*. "Now, let's say 'ol Buck decides to give his guests a little bonus. What would you think a *second* destination for a family sailing vacation might be?" he asked.

82

"The Les Cheneaux Islands?" Pete guessed.

"Maybe," Eddie said, "but it's probably too shallow for a seventy-foot, two-masted schooner. No, not the Snows, but I think you're going in the right direction."

"Mackinac Island," Dan breathed. There was an excitement in his voice that Pete didn't comprehend at first.

"An unchartered trip here for a day would be very welcome to a family—say with two kids who are bored out of their skulls with scenery and would just love to ride horses for an afternoon. It could fit perfectly with some sort of illegal scheme that Buck might be up to," Kate added. "On paper, the two boats never come close to each other. But with Herman as the go-between here, they would be in contact every week."

"That's kind of what I thought, too," Eddie said, scratching out his sand map.

The four went back to their bikes and finished their ride around the island, three of them eagerly awaiting the next step in their adventure—the fourth, agonizing at the very thought of it.

Sleeping In

CHAPTER 15
THE PLAN

Dinner that evening with Mr. and Mrs. Anderson was another feast. Chef Zachary had prepared a lamb and rice dish in orange gravy that was beyond words. For Pete, that was terrific, but even better was that the conversation never got around to Herman, Buck and the two boats. Unfortunately, it wasn't because his friends had forgotten—they just didn't want to bring it up in front of the Andersons, who would surely put an end to the enterprise if they had even a clue what the kids were up to. So, after dessert, the four stood, excused themselves and went to the Straits Room. Kate quickly spread some books and maps on the large, round table.

"All you're doing here is guessing," Pete said. "Herman might just simply be a down on his luck bum. We have no proof that he's working with the *Quince* or the *V.A. Frazier*."

"You're right," Eddie said, "but when you put a puzzle together, even if some of the pieces are missing, what you see is probably what the picture will be."

"And we've got a lot of the pieces," Dan agreed.

"It sure looks like something funny is going on."

"It all seems too far-fetched," Pete said.

"I'd agree," Kate said, "if we hadn't found that shipping schedule in Herman's box with the *Quince* and the *V.A. Frazier* underlined."

"What would keep Herman from just taking the money he gets and leaving Mackinac—never to be seen again?" Pete argued.

"I don't know," Dan answered. "But according to Mr. Colesmith, Buck Meesley's got Herman's number."

"If this is so clear, why don't you tell your aunt and uncle?" Pete said.

"We still don't have any *real* proof," said Kate. "We're not sure what they're doing, who they're doing it with . . . "

"But we've seen enough to know that they're dangerous," Pete argued.

"Nothing's going to happen," Kate reassured him.

"It's dark now," said Dan. "I'll bet Herman is getting ready to row back here from Round Island. I wonder where he keeps his boat."

"Here or there?" Eddie asked.

"Both," Dan said. "We walked the whole shore of Round Island this morning and didn't see it."

"We weren't looking for a boat," Eddie said.

"That's right and it could be kept anywhere here on Mackinac," Kate added, "under the boardwalk, by the coal dock, over at Mission Point—anywhere."

"I've had enough for one day," Pete said with a yawn. "I'm going to bed."

"Me too," Dan said. "We'll want an early start tomorrow."

———

At seven A.M. a tap came at Pete's door.

"Come on, Pete. Everyone's dressed and

86

downstairs." It was Dan.

Pete opened his eyes. The crisp morning air made him want to slide back under the covers. The bright, sunny sky and the full night's sleep, on the other hand, made him want to bound out of bed. The slide-back-under-the-covers won out momentarily, but as he was drawing the quilt around him, he remembered Kate.

He wished sometimes that he wasn't so taken with her. But he was. Any chance he could be with her he would plunge into headfirst. Right now, she was waiting for him at breakfast—doing something else he could never resist: eating warm pastries and fresh fruit. He was out of bed and into his clothes before he could change his mind.

It wasn't until he sat down at the Straits Room table and saw the sun rising above the Round Island Lighthouse that he remembered the whole Herman-and-Buck deal.

"Good morning, Pete," Kate said. "Did you sleep okay?"

"Like a bunny in a burrow. How about you?—none of your weird dreams, I hope."

"No, nothing like that," Kate said. "I wish you were more excited about our adventure."

"It just seems that we might be getting ourselves in a real pickle," Pete said.

"Sometimes I think you'd be afraid of your own shadow," Kate taunted.

"My shadow hardly ever throws knives or plays with chicken blood," Pete reminded her. Looking over toward Dan and Eddie, he asked, "So, what's our plan?"

"If we're right," Dan said, "and Herman waited until the middle of the night to row across from Round Island, then he's probably sleeping in this morning."

"We want to get into his barn when he's not there," Eddie said, "so we figure he'll get up around noon and

87

then, with some of the money we saw in his stash box, he'll go into town and get something to eat."

"If we tee off from Wawashkamo at eleven," Dan continued, "that would get us to the seventh hole at about 12:30. Eddie's drive should put us at Herman's doorstep a few minutes later. If he's not yelling at us, we can assume he's not there. Then we check the stick that Kate put at his barn door to see if it's been moved. If it has, it means he's been there and gone. If so, we go in to see what's in the box."

"Sounds like a lot of *ifs* to me," Pete said, picking up his juice glass. "What if one of your guesses is wrong? What if we stumble inside and find ourselves facing a madman with a handful of razor-sharp daggers?"

"Yes, that would be bad, all right," Kate said, getting up. "Well, let's go."

Pete choked on his orange juice. "`Let's go'? What do you mean `Let's go'? What about the knives?"

"Relax, Pete," Kate said. "Nothing's going to happen. You'll see."

Kate's Drives Were Long And Straight

CHAPTER 16
MASHIES AND NIBLICKS

By noon the sun was beating down on the Mackinac Island golf course. A week had passed since any rain had fallen and heat waves were radiating from the hardened brown fairways. Only the tees and greens, which were watered regularly, showed any sign of life.

The golfers approached the seventh tee, playing as they had the day before, with Kate and Pete paired against Dan and Eddie. Pete had learned the names of all the clubs from the driver to the putter, which he already knew, but also, among others, the mashie, the niblick and the mashie-niblick. He learned which club to use when the ball was varying distances from the pin—not that it ever went as far as it was supposed to. His putts were often longer than his mashies . . . or his niblicks . . . or even his mashie-niblicks.

"It's just like shooting free throws in basketball," Dan explained to Pete. "You learn the right stroke and then you repeat it."

That was all well and good, except the ball never

89

landed on the same type of ground twice in a row. Sometimes it would roll to the bottom of a hollow in deep grass and he would have to bend way over to hit it. Or else it would come to rest on a sandy ledge practically at eye level and he'd have to swing at it as if it were perched on a baseball tee. No two strokes were ever the same. The sport was impossible. Still, he was with Kate and for that, Pete, armed only with his backspin-mashie, would walk through an entire sand trap filled with massasauga rattlesnakes.

One interesting thing happened. On the fourth hole Kate chipped her second shot to the apron way at the back of the green—a full seventy feet from the pin. They were at best two and quite possibly three putts from holing out. Dan and Eddie smirked as Dan's third shot rolled up four inches from the cup. A par would put them in the lead.

Pete stood nervously as he lined up the long, down hill, seventy-footer. He smacked it hard—way too hard. The ball went left, then right and then gaining speed, it went straight for the cup. By the time it approached the hole, it was really moving. This would surely have been one of Pete's longest shots of the day, drives included, had it not rolled directly over the cup, caught the back lip and popped about two feet in the air. It dropped to the green, teetered for a moment on the edge of the hole and fell *kerplunk* right in the bottom. Birdie!

Kate nearly unglued. She ran to Pete, grabbed him around the neck with both arms and gave him a kiss he wouldn't soon forget. She then grabbed his hand in hers and the two marched to the fifth tee, striding past Dan and Eddie, who remained on the green, staring blankly at their four-inch putt.

At the end of six holes the score, once again, was even. As they moved to the seventh tee, everyone's eyes were drawn to the left rough where the old barn stood deep in the woods. This was it—the Avon call at Herman's door. Eddie teed up, took a deep breath and crushed the ball. It shot on a beeline toward the green. At about the point his drives normally began their slow curve to the left, the ball instead continued straight for the flag. It landed on the concrete-hard battleground and bounced another two hundred yards, coming to rest twenty feet from the green.

"Oh, too bad," Dan said smiling. "Try this one." He flipped another ball to his partner.

"If only I could do that when I wanted," Eddie said. He placed the new ball carefully on another sand pile, stepped back and whacked it. Again, it flew off the tee down the fairway. But this time, to no one's real surprise, it began the same graceful high-arching loop to the left that had led the golfers into the woods the day before. The ball cleared the cedars and disappeared from sight. A moment later the four were rewarded with a loud, hollow thud that would have awakened an 1814 Major Holmes statue.

"That's better," Dan said. "Let's go for a walk."

The foursome shouldered their bags and strode together down the fairway. At a break in the dense cedar brush, they veered into the rough. Dan led the way, with Eddie, Kate and Pete following.

To Pete's delight, there was no one around.

"I think it went in over this tree," Dan said loudly enough for anyone in the area to hear. "Look, there's a barn."

"It sounded like your ball might have hit it," Kate said, also projecting her voice. "Let's check there."

Kate went to the door and looked for the twig. She pointed to where she expected it to be and whispered to the others, "The stick's been moved."

"The ball must have hit this wall," Eddie said, straining his voice, again for the benefit of Herman. "Spread out. It's got to be nearby."

The four moved around the outside of the barn. Their heads were down as they pretended to look for Eddie's ball. Each of them nervously expected to see Herman LeRoux jump out from the old structure.

Soon the golfers met again at the barn door. "Well, if it isn't outside, maybe it's inside," Kate said to anyone within a quarter of a mile of the barn. "It could have gone right through one of those old boards." She waited a few moments, giving Herman time to show himself. When he didn't, she moved toward the entrance. Dan and Eddie set their golf bags on the ground next to Kate's and went inside, following her step for step. Pete remained near the edge of the fairway until the other three had entered the barn. He then hurried to catch up with them.

"I don't see your ball on the floor, Eddie," Kate said, her voice raised.

"Maybe it landed up in that loft," Dan called out. "There's a ladder. I'll check to see where it goes."

Pete, from his place at the doorway, watched for any sign of movement above. He was ready to give warning and be gone in an instant. But nothing happened, not even when Dan made his way to the top rung and peeked over the edge.

Dan turned his eyes back to his friends on the barn floor. "He's not up here," he whispered. "Eddie, help me look around. Kate, you and Pete stand guard outside in case Herman comes back."

That suited Pete just fine. "Let's go, Kate," he said. "We'll make like we're looking for the ball."

"If he comes," Kate said, "yell, `I found it,' like someone is back on the fairway."

"Okay, you do the same," Pete said. "I'll take this

side of the barn. You take the other."

"No, Pete," Kate said. "You keep a lookout for Herman. *I'm* going up to the loft."

"What? I can't watch both sides at once," Pete protested.

"Sure you can," Kate said as she turned to go inside. "Besides, Herman is probably sitting in some restaurant in town right now. If he does come, you know what to do. Call out to us and then try to hold him off."

"Right," Pete said with as much bravado as he could muster. What was he going to stall this knife-throwing madman with?—his niblick?

Kate went inside and up the ladder. In seconds, she was beside Dan and Eddie as they searched for Herman's box.

"He must have put it in a different place," said Dan.

"I wonder if he used the same trick we did," Eddie said. "You know, leaving a stick where we wouldn't notice it."

"Maybe," Kate said, "but if he did, we're too late to do anything about it. We've probably already moved it. Keep looking."

"Wait a minute," said Eddie. He was standing on his tip-toes and reaching up on a crossbeam. "I can feel something."

SNAP!

"YEOW!" Eddie hollered. He pulled his arm down and stared at a rat trap clamped firmly to the three middle fingers on his right hand. Dan pried the bar back and Eddie shook some circulation into his stinging fingertips.

Hearing Eddie's yell, Pete ran to the barn door. "What was that?" Pete called softly.

"Nothing important," Kate said. "Eddie just found a mouse trap. Keep watching for Herman."

"'Mouse trap' nothing," Eddie said, still rubbing his hand. "That was a *rat* trap and if it had been *your* fingers, I bet you wouldn't have thought it was 'nothing important.'"

Kate was on her hands and knees working herself into a tight corner where the roof slanted down almost to the wall of the barn. "Here it is," she said. She grabbed the box and inched her way back to where she could stand next to Dan and Eddie. She snapped the clasp and all three looked inside.

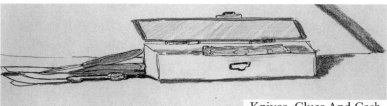

CHAPTER 17
THE LIST

When the lid popped open a thick stack of twenty-dollar bills greeted their eyes.

"How much do you think there is now?" Kate breathed.

"A lot more than yesterday. Maybe five thousand," Eddie said, fanning the money.

"I want to see what else there is," Dan said. He reached into the box and withdrew four perfectly balanced daggers. He set them aside and pulled out a skeleton key. He turned it over in his hands before setting it back in the box. Next, he removed a folded piece of paper. "I didn't see any of this stuff yesterday," he said, opening the sheet.

Eddie peeked over Dan's shoulder. "It's just a bunch of initials," Eddie said, looking at the paper.

"Right," Kate agreed, "but it must mean something."

From below, they heard a voice. It was Pete. "Is this your ball, Eddie?—a Wilson Two?"

"I can't believe he's yelling so loud to tell me that he found my ball," Eddie said.

Kate stiffened. "No!" she said. "That's our signal. Someone's coming." She started to return the box to its hiding place.

"Leave it here, Kate!" Dan said. "We've got to get downstairs fast!"

Pete had heard something moving through the woods on the other side of the barn. At first he thought it must be a deer, but then he remembered Dan saying that no large game animals lived on the island. It had to be Herman! Instantly, Pete called out the warning. He raced around to the other side and stood in the clearing in front of the barn door. He'd stall Herman for as long as he could.

Moments later, an unbelievably grimy, rough-looking man with long, black hair appeared from the woods.

"Hey, who are you?" Herman LeRoux shouted. He reached for a knife sheathed in a scabbard tied just below his right knee. He stepped into the clearing and the dagger's eight-inch blade glistened in the sun. He flipped it in the air and caught the tip with his thumb and forefinger, snapping it into throwing position. "What you doin' here?"

"Looking for a golf ball," Pete gulped, holding it in front of him. "My friend hit it into the rough. I just found it." Pete could hear sounds from inside the barn and knew that Herman had, also. It would do no good to pretend that no one was there. He just hoped they had recognized his signal and come down from the loft. Pete tried to think of a way to delay the man, but he knew that sooner or later, Herman would rush in.

"Who's in my barn?" Herman bellowed, starting for the door.

"Just my friends," Pete said. "They looked all around outside and thought it might have gone through the roof and landed inside."

Herman kept the knife aimed at Pete's chest as he rushed toward the rundown building. He yanked the door open. There, standing together, were Kate, Dan and Eddie.

96

"Hi," Kate said, forcing a smile. "Can we help you?"

"What you doin' snoopin' roun' my barn, eh?" Herman LeRoux shouted.

"*Your* barn?" Kate said, looking aghast. "We're terribly sorry. Eddie, here, hit a ball out of bounds. We came to look for it and found this old shed. We thought it was just an abandoned building." Again she smiled casually. "Well, I guess Pete found the ball, so I suppose we'll go back to our game."

"I s'pose you'll wait right here till I check sumpin' out," Herman said with a snarl. "You," he pointed the butt of his knife toward Pete. "You go first. Any of my stuff is missin' an' all four o' you is gonna lose a lot more'n a golf ball."

He directed Pete toward the ladder and motioned him to climb. Hand over hand, Pete pulled himself up the rungs to the loft. Immediately, he noticed the open box. He then turned and stood overlooking the scene of his three terrified friends and the desperate thief standing below. Herman started up the rungs keeping one hand on the knife. He glanced at Pete and then turned his head and stared at the three others below, making sure they weren't trying to make a run for it.

When Herman looked down, Pete saw his chance. He dropped silently, feet first, from the loft. His heels struck Herman's skull with a bone-jarring crash. The knife flew from Herman's hand and the two plummeted to the ground. Pete jumped to his feet as Herman groaned in agony on the barn floor.

"Let's get out of here!" Pete yelled.

He could have saved his breath. His friends were already out the door. Pete followed as they grabbed their clubs and ran toward the fairway. They didn't stop until they reached the Wawashkamo Clubhouse practice green.

97

There, they slowed to a walk and caught their breath.

"What made you think to jump Herman like that?" Kate finally asked.

"When I got to the loft and saw the open box, I knew that once Herman got to the top of the ladder, he would know you had found it. I figured we'd be goners for sure. So, when he turned his eyes away from me, I jumped."

"That was the bravest thing I've ever seen," Eddie said. "You saved our lives."

"Yeah, well, mine too," Pete said. "It was sort of a self-preservation thing—something I've been getting a lot of practice at lately."

Dan was walking ahead of the others, deep in thought. "The *V.A. Frazier* and the *Quince* come by here only every week or so," he said. "I wonder what Herman does when he's not rowing back and forth to the lighthouse."

"He doesn't seem to be working anywhere," said Kate.

"I doubt if he's involved in much charity work—church socials and the like," Eddie said with a laugh.

"I don't think he's much of a reader," Pete said. "I didn't see any books lying around in his loft."

"You can be sure he doesn't spend any time grooming himself," Kate said. "That's the filthiest person I've ever seen."

"So, what do you think he does?" Dan asked.

"Let's see if Ginny is at the <u>Town Crier</u>," Kate suggested. "Maybe she's heard something that hasn't made the paper."

The four hurried into the Wawashkamo Clubhouse and turned in their bags. They hopped on their bikes and started back to town.

Mrs. Hurst's Emerald Bracelet

CHAPTER 18
CAT BURGLAR

Kate led the others into the <u>Town Crier</u> office. Ginny Lind glanced up from the article she was writing for her "Kids' Kolumn" of the weekly paper.

"What's new?" Ginny asked.

"Plenty," Kate replied. "And we need your help. That Herman LeRoux-guy you told us about?—we think he's part of some smuggling ring. We don't know what he's dealing in or how he's doing it, but he's got about four thousand dollars more than he did yesterday."

"Have you heard about anything going on that he might be mixed up in?" Dan asked.

"Now that you mention it," Ginny said, "this morning an East Bluff cottager came into the office and told my dad that his wife has been missing some jewelry for over a week. Now that in itself would hardly be enough to get excited about, but she's not the only one. It happened to someone from the West Bluff only two days ago. Olivia Hurst is in a real lather over an emerald bracelet that she was sure she had left on her vanity table."

"Did you say Olivia Hurst?" Dan gasped.

"Yes, why?" Ginny asked, surprised at Dan's reaction.

"Because Olivia Hurst is Denton Hurst's wife. That explains the note I found in Herman's box. There was a whole list of initials—some of them crossed off. D.H. was the last one with a line through it."

"What was the next one?" Kate asked.

Dan was lost in thought. "Please?" he said finally.

"If D.H. was the last one with a line through it, what were the next initials that hadn't been checked off?" Kate asked.

"Oh, uh, I don't know," Dan said. "D.H. only caught my eye because it's my own initials. I was trying to figure out what the letters had to do with the boats on the shipping schedule. None made any sense. But now, it's obvious! Denton Hurst's cottage is part of Herman's list of burglary targets."

"This changes everything," Eddie said.

"It sure does," Kate agreed. "First of all, it means that Herman isn't simply a go-between for Buck and the guy aboard the *V.A. Frazier*. Herman *is* the thief. He may even be the brains behind the whole scheme."

"Let's not get carried away," Eddie said. "One look at Herman LeRoux and `brainy' is hardly a word you'd use to describe him."

"Think hard," Ginny urged. "What were some of the other initials?"

Dan closed his eyes. He finally shook his head. "No good. I can't remember any of them."

"Well, I guess that leaves just one thing for us to do," Kate said.

"Drop the whole thing?" Pete said hopefully.

"No," said Kate, ignoring Pete's suggestion. "We've got to go back to Herman's barn and find that list. It will tell us who he has robbed—that will prove our case—and it will also tell us where he plans on breaking into next."

"You must be joking!" Pete said. "He'd kill us!"

"We'll just have to be more careful," said Dan. "But Kate's right. We have to get those names."

"So, if Herman *is* doing the stealing, who wrote the list?" Kate asked.

"Good question," Dan said. "The handwriting wasn't anything like the warning message to us on Round Island."

"The initials in Herman's stash box were done in blue ink," Eddie said, "but they were crossed off with thick, black pencil marks—the same kind of lead that was used on the note in the dinghy."

Kate looked at Ginny. "Who else has had things stolen?" she asked.

"Mostly East Bluff people," Ginny answered. "Denton Hurst's cottage was the only one so far on the West Bluff."

"Isn't the West Bluff where your aunt and uncle live?" Pete asked Dan.

"The Hursts are only three doors away," Dan nodded.

"Do you think Mr. and Mrs. Anderson have heard about the robberies?" Eddie asked.

"I don't know," Kate said. "It's not as if they meet at the well every night and chat like Pete's family and neighbors do in the Snows."

"It's almost noon," said Dan. "We'll ask Aunt and Uncle over lunch."

"Will you be here at the newspaper office this afternoon, Ginny?" Kate asked.

"Most of the time," Ginny said. "But if you hear anything, let me know. Don't even think about leaving me out of this. A jewelry bust would be the biggest story of the summer and I want the scoop."

———

Nancy and George Anderson smiled as their four guests gathered for sandwiches. "What have you kids been up to today?" Mrs. Anderson asked.

"We went golfing this morning," Kate said.

"So I hear," George Anderson said. "Mr. Dennis

told me you set a course record for the quickest nine holes ever."

"We were playing partners so it went pretty fast," Dan said.

"We heard in town that some cottages have been broken into," Kate said. "Do you know anything about it?"

"Only rumors," Mrs. Anderson said. "Olivia Hurst thinks she is missing a bracelet, but she could be mistaken."

"If you lost, say, a diamond pin," Kate said to Aunt Nancy, "how soon do you think you would realize it was gone?"

"If someone was going to break into our house," Uncle George said, "he wouldn't steal a pin or a bracelet. He'd take a whole jewelry box. We would miss that right away. Why do you ask?"

"Oh, nothing," Kate said. "We were just talking to Ginny Lind at the <u>Town Crier</u>. It seems, with no police here anymore, people have been coming to her father to ask about such things. It's as if he has become the complaint department for the whole Island."

"I think the town council needs to get a replacement for Chief Chamberlain," George Anderson said.

"And soon," Aunt Nancy added. "I don't like the thought of someone breaking into homes and there is no one to report it to, even if these are only rumors."

Just then the phone rang in the living room.

"I'll get it," Kate said, jumping to her feet.

A moment later she returned. "It was Ginny. She says to meet her at the yacht dock."

"What's it's about?" Dan asked.

"I don't know," Kate said. "But she wants us to come right away."

"The *Quince*, In Person."

CHAPTER 19
PURSUIT

The four filed out the back door and ran to the horse barn. They grabbed their bikes and raced down the hill. In ten minutes they were pulling up to the marina. Moored at the far end of the dock was an antique, two-masted schooner.

"Could that be the *Quince*?" Kate wondered.

Ginny stepped from behind the dockmaster's office. "In person," she said. "She came in half an hour ago. A family of four got off and went ashore. I watched them hire a Carriage Tours hack, so they'll be gone for two hours at least. After they left, the *Quince's* captain came up to the dock and I followed him into town. He was standing outside Doud's Grocery when he glanced around to see if anyone was watching. He looked my way and I ducked behind the water fountain. And the next moment he grabbed a silver-and-blue Schwinn. It was an `Orr Kids' rental bike. He raced up the hill and turned onto Market Street. I ran to the office, phoned you, then came back here." Ginny stepped toward the *Quince*. "Let's see what's aboard."

"If Buck Meesley is meeting Herman at his barn, we have at least an hour before he'll be back," Dan said as he followed Ginny to the schooner's gangplank.

Eddie stepped back. "I'm not boarding someone's boat uninvited," he said.

"Why not?" Ginny asked.

"You just don't *do* that," Eddie said.

"You didn't mind going into Herman's barn," Kate reminded him.

"That's different" Eddie said. "It's not really Herman's. It's abandoned. This boat *belongs* to someone. Besides, Buck probably buttoned her up pretty good. I say we go to the barn and try to hear what they're up to."

"Okay," Dan said. "But we'd better hurry."

———

Up the hill the five went, this time not stopping at Wawashkamo Club House but pedaling along British Landing Road past the seventh tee.

"No one is on the fairway," Dan said. "Follow me."

Dan rode his bike off the road over the hard turf. He laid the two-wheeler down softly in the tall grass of the left rough. The others followed and silently slipped through the cedar brush. Twenty yards from the barn stood a silver-and-blue Schwinn with *Orr Kids* painted in purple on the back fender.

"That's the bike Buck Meesley stole," Ginny whispered. "He must be in the barn."

"I can't hear anything," Eddie said.

"We've got to get closer," Kate whispered.

"I hope you don't mean *inside*," Pete said.

"No, but if we go around to the back, we would be directly beneath the loft," Dan said. "We might be able to hear them from there." Dan led the way into the clearing and darted around to the back of the run-down building.

He put an ear to the wall to listen.

A man's voice yelled gruffly from above, "This is it? This is all we got? A lousy five grand? There's enough ice on this island to make us rich forever. If you're holdin' back on me, Herman, you'll wish you hadn't."

"No, Buck, honest. I gotta be careful," another voice pleaded. It was Herman, but he didn't sound nearly as bold as when he had been pointing his knife at four kids in golf clothes. "People here are startin' t' get wise. I heard at the Mustang today that the old lady on the West Bluff found out her bracelet was gone."

"Then you'd better make your next job the last," the first voice said. "And I don't mean take just one or two pieces, eh? I mean clean it out—jewelry, silverware, cash—the works. Sam don't come by for three days and I'm castin' off in the *Quince* in two hours. You can case the job now and we'll do it together on the night the *V.A. Frazier* comes through. Listen up. This here's the place I been savin' for last."

The sun beat down on the five teens as they listened, but Buck's gruff voice was no longer shouting. As Pete leaned closer a blade of grass bristled deep inside his nose. He pulled back but it was too late. Water was flowing into his eyes and the sneeze was well on its way.

"Ah . . . aah . . . aaah . . . CHOO!" Pete's head nearly exploded. He fell backwards, tripping on a log. He sneezed again. He tried to get to his feet but fell once more. Again he sneezed. When he opened his eyes, his four friends were running toward the fairway. From the edge of the woods Kate stopped and waved frantically for Pete to hurry, but he froze when he heard the two thieves inside the barn scrambling down the ladder. They burst through the doorway, spied Kate standing in the distance and took off after her.

Kate seeing Buck and Herman running toward her, ducked into the underbrush, grabbed her bike and raced to catch up with Dan, Eddie and Ginny, who were already halfway across the seventh fairway.

The two men ran onto the golf course but could do nothing except watch the four bikers disappear around a curve in British Landing Road.

———

"We can't leave Pete alone," Kate said as the four coasted to a stop.

"I've got an idea," Dan said. "We'll circle around behind the golf clubhouse on State Road and hope he comes out that way."

———

Pete watched Buck and Herman chase Kate onto the golf course and before considering the consequences, he dashed into the barn. He scrambled up the ladder and found the open green box in the loft where Buck and Herman had left it. An old key sat atop the coveted sheet of paper. Pete picked up the key and absent-mindedly slipped it in his hip pocket as he reached for the note.

He stared intently, memorizing three initials with lines through them and three without. Another was circled, so he committed that to memory, too. Holding the note, an ominous feeling came over him that he was about to be caught. He set the paper back in the box and slid down the ladder. As he was about to run out of the barn, he heard someone nearby.

"You idiot!" shouted a gruff voice. It was Buck. "Why didn't you tell me about those four little creeps?"

"They're just kids," Herman said weakly. "I chased 'em off this morning when I caught 'em lookin' for golf balls. They don't know nothin'."

"Maybe not this mornin'," Buck yelled, "but they weren't lookin' for no golf balls this afternoon. They was

106

snoopin'—listenin' in on our plans. If they heard *anything*, they know too much."

Pete cringed inside the barn as the two argued but a few yards away. *If I make a run for it*, Pete thought, *I wouldn't get two steps before I have a knife in my back. I've got to hide here and pray that they leave.* Pete moved silently into a dark corner behind the door.

"You sure they was the same kids you seen this mornin'?" Buck demanded.

"Yeah, except then I thought it was three boys and one girl," Herman said. "Just now it looked more like two and two."

Buck glanced a few feet away into the tall grass and saw Pete's bicycle. "What's this?" he hollered. "They all rode off on bikes, right?"

"Yeah," Herman said. "All four of 'em."

"Then there must be another one!" Buck yelled. "This here's a boy's bike—he must be aroun' somewheres!"

Buck slammed the two-wheeler to the ground as he scanned the area. His eyes fell on the barn.

Pete crammed himself further into the corner as he watched Buck run directly toward him.

Buck charged into the barn and stopped. He listened intently as he stared toward the loft.

Pete was so near he could hear Buck's heavy breathing. He could sense his anger—even smell his rage. If Pete made the faintest rustle, Buck would whirl and be on him in a flash. He would crush Pete's ribs and backbone with one murderous bear hug.

Herman ran into the barn and stood at Buck's side. Buck raised his hand for Herman to keep still.

"He's up there," Buck whispered. "I know he is. And he's got your knives. They're in the box, right!"

"Well, yeah, some of them," Herman muttered.

"Why?"

"If he's found 'em, he could slice us up good before we even got over the edge!" Buck bellowed. "He could hold us off until his pals get back with help. I'd force him out with fire but then our five thousand bucks would go up in smoke, too. We've got to rush him now. Since they're your knives you left layin' around, you can go first."

Herman glanced at Buck and then looked anxiously toward the loft. He knew how sharp those blades were and how easily they could be thrown. He moved to the ladder and slowly pulled himself up the rungs. When he reached the top he peered over the edge. Silently, he crawled onto the loft floor and sprang to his feet. Crouching nervously, his eyes darted in all directions. Finally, he straightened and sighed a breath of relief.

"He ain't up here," Herman called to Buck.

"Is the box still there?" Buck yelled.

Herman turned to the open case. "Yeah," he called out as he reached down for his daggers, "just like we left it."

Buck started quickly up the ladder.

From behind the door Pete could see that neither of the men were looking his way. As quietly as he could, he dashed outside. He had gone no more than twenty feet when he stepped on a twig. With blood pounding in his head, Pete didn't hear the telltale snap of the broken limb.

But Buck did.

"That's him!" Buck yelled. From halfway up the ladder, he jumped to the ground, landing with his powerful legs churning full stride for the barn door.

Pete's Escape

CHAPTER 20
ESCAPE

As Pete hurried toward the woods he heard Buck's furious yell. In blind terror, Pete ran like never before. Ahead of him was the forest with what appeared to be an open trail going through it. Suddenly he noticed the silver-and-blue Schwinn.

That's Buck's, he remembered. As he continued to run, he grabbed the handlebars, righted the bike and glanced backwards toward the barn. There, charging into the doorway, was Buck. In the next moment, Herman LeRoux appeared at Buck's side. Herman drew a knife from his leg scabbard and raised it into throwing position.

Pete turned and made a running leap onto the two-wheeler. Before he could put his feet on the pedals he heard a thud in the tree to his left. A quick glance showed Herman's blade quivering in the trunk six inches from his head. Pete pedaled for all he was worth and crested a hill five yards away.

He pumped hard twice before, *Ching!* a second dagger glanced off his shoe and tore into the sprocket.

The chain snapped but, luckily, Pete was on the down slope of a steep hill. The bicycle picked up speed and went fifty yards before the broken chain flew off its cogs. It jammed in the front wheel and stopped the bike as if it had smashed into a brick wall.

"Aaaiiee!" Pete screamed as he instantly went airborne, hurtling high over the handlebars. He saw the trunk of a huge oak tree approaching, as if in slow motion, straight for his face. He twisted his body and barely scraped the tree, landing in the soft dirt. His scream echoed through the forest.

———

"What was that?" Kate shrieked as she led the four bikers along the back road.

"It came from just around the bend!" Dan cried.

"It's Pete! He must be hurt!" Kate yelled. "Hurry!"

The four pumped hard around the curve and up a sharp hill. Just ahead they saw Pete kneeling in the road, the silver-and-blue Schwinn crumpled in a heap behind him. They spun their bikes around and hurried to head back to him.

"Are you all right?" Kate asked.

"So far," Pete panted, "but we've got to get out of here. Herman and Buck are right behind me!"

"Hop on," Eddie said.

Dan turned and saw the two men running in the distance toward them. "They're coming!" he yelled.

Pete jumped onto Eddie's handlebars. The bikers sped down the hill and around the bend, putting the forest between themselves and the two thieves.

Buck and Herman rushed to the fallen bicycle, but their prey had vanished.

———

"What's the matter?" Mr. Dennis asked as the five

stormed up the path to the Wawashkamo clubhouse.

Dan yelled, "Call my uncle! Tell him it was Herman LeRoux and Buck Meesley. They might be trying to get away aboard the *Quince*."

"Whoa, slow down," Mr. Dennis said. "What's the *Quince*?"

"It's an old schooner!" Kate said. "We're going down to the marina right now to warn the people who chartered her."

"Hold on a second," Mr. Dennis said. "Who are Buck Meesley and Herman LeRoux?"

"Jewel thieves!" Kate said. "They've been stealing from Mackinac cottagers all summer. One of them threw a knife at Pete and nearly killed him." She ran toward a bicycle rack holding several two-wheelers. "We need a bike. Which one can we use?"

"Take mine," Mr. Dennis said, pointing to an English three-speed.

———

"You idiot!" Buck Meesley yelled.

"I couldn't just let 'em get away," Herman cried. "They know everything. I had to try to stop 'em. All your planning, all the jobs I pulled, all Sam's dealin' with the guy in Chicago—all lost on account of them golf-playin' rich kids. Don't you see? I couldn't let 'em just pedal off down the road and blab to the cops."

"Yeah, you're right," Buck said. "But now I gotta make some new plans. We got a little dough, but not enough. Maybe them kids don't know no more than that some guy just threw a knife at one of 'em. Maybe we can still take the *Quince* off the Island and get away."

"Yeah, Buck," Herman said. "Let's try for it. Just because they was here this mornin' snoopin' aroun' don't mean they're on to us."

"You sure they're the same kids?" Buck asked.

111

"Yeah, they might even be the ones I seen yesterday on Round Island. I bashed up their little party over there. They was scopin' out the old lighthouse and I didn't want 'em gettin' too used to hangin' aroun'."

Buck stared at Herman in disbelief. "What? You sure? You seen the same kids on Round Island?"

Herman shrugged. "Yeah. So?"

"Then we are in trouble," Buck said slowly. "If they knew you was the one that messed with 'em over there, then that's why they followed you here today. And I'll bet they got some idea of what's goin' on with the *Quince*, too. Now, keep quiet till I figger out what to do."

———

Five minutes later Buck looked at Herman. "Did any of 'em get upstairs?" he asked. "Did any of 'em see what was inside the box?—get a look at the maps?"

"No, Buck. Nobody got up there," Herman said. "They couldn't have. They'd have grabbed the money."

Buck thought for a moment and then nodded. "Yeah, I guess. Okay, go get the box," Buck said. "We gotta clear outta here 'fore the cops come."

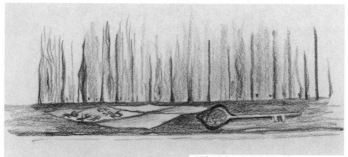
Hit List And Skeleton Key

CHAPTER 21
THE LIST

The five bikers sped away from Wawashkamo down the hill.

"Ginny," Dan said to the girl riding beside him, "is your father at the <u>Town Crier</u> now?"

"Probably," she said. "Why?"

"We'll need some help with these guys," Dan said. "We won't be able to stop Buck and Herman if they decide to board the *Quince* and cast off."

"If they know what's good for them, they won't even try," Kate said. "The Coast Guard would head them off before they got out of the harbor."

"Maybe Buck and Herman don't realize we know about the *Quince*," Pete said.

"They must think by now that we were following Herman," Dan said. "Herman's seen us three times already. If he hasn't figured it out, Buck surely will."

"They might wait and take the *Quince* out tonight," Pete said.

"There aren't very many nineteenth-century schooners around the Lakes," Eddie said. "The *Quince* would stick out like a donkey at the Derby. They'd get caught sooner or later."

"How come you didn't try to catch up with us after you sneezed, Pete?" Eddie asked as he coasted his bike down the long, slow grade of Hoban Road.

"I kept falling down and by the time I could get up, I heard Buck and Herman coming down the ladder," Pete said. "I'd have run right into them as they came out the door."

"So, what did you do while they were chasing us?" Kate asked.

"I knew how much you wanted that list, so when I saw them following you out on the golf course, I decided I'd have time to go inside the barn and find it."

Kate nearly veered off the road as she stared at Pete in amazement. "You *what?*" she said.

"I thought if I could find that sheet and memorize a few of the initials, we might warn the people so they wouldn't get robbed," Pete said calmly.

"It's a wonder you didn't get caught up there," Ginny said.

"Yeah, I guess it was pretty stupid," Pete agreed.

"'Stupid' nothing," Kate said. "That's the most daring thing I've ever heard."

"Sometimes 'daring' and 'stupid' are the same thing," Pete said.

Kate considered that for a moment. "I suppose," she said. "Anyway, did you find the note?"

"Yep," Pete said.

"You're kidding! Do you remember the initials?" Kate persisted.

"I think so," said Pete. "I put them in sort of a rhyme. Three of the ones with lines through them were H.V., A.G. and C.B."

Ginny Lind knew all the Mackinac residents, year-round and seasonal. She quickly filled in the names. "Henry Vanderbilt, Abner Getty and Cyrus Briggs," she

114

said. "All wealthy East Bluff cottagers—and all reported missing jewelry."

"Three that weren't crossed off were B.K., W.A. and R.J.," Pete added.

"Bernard Kroger, Walter Appleby and Ramsey Jackson," Ginny continued. "All on the West Bluff and none with any thefts reported."

"One other was circled," Pete said.

"Really?" Dan said anxiously, "what was it?"

"G.A." Pete said.

"George Anderson," Dan whispered. "Uncle George."

"I'll bet they were planning on Aunt and Uncle's place for their final job," Kate said.

"Could be," Dan agreed, "but they must know better than trying anything like that now."

As he rode along, Pete felt something uncomfortable in his left hip pocket. He reached back and pulled out a skeleton key. Remembering where it had come from, he showed it to Kate. "I found this in the box, too."

"What could that old thing go to?" Kate asked.

"Around here?" Ginny said, glancing over, "as old as the buildings are, it might work on any of them."

"I saw it in the box this morning," Dan said, "but it wasn't there yesterday. Herman must have had it with him on Round Island."

"Do you think it's the key to the lighthouse?" Kate asked. "I remember looking at the keyhole when we were there. It wasn't a modern lock, I know that much."

The five bikers picked up speed as they approached Grand Hill. Soon they were flying past carriages, tourists and street sweepers. After making the left turn at Market Street, Kate and Ginny stopped at the Town Crier office.

115

"You guys go ahead," Kate said. "Ginny and I will talk to Mr. Lind and then meet you at the yacht dock."

"We'll be aboard the *M·I·S·T*," Dan said. "It's close enough to the *Quince* that we can watch for Herman and Buck if they try to get away. I'm sure they couldn't have beat us down here. We had a pretty good head start."

"And I know for a fact that silver and blue Schwinn is out of commission," Pete said.

"That's true," Eddie said, "but they might have found your bike, Pete. They could be riding double like we did. They might even have beaten us. We *did* stop at the clubhouse."

"We'll hurry," said Kate as she followed Ginny into the newspaper office.

The three boys continued to the yacht dock and boarded the *M·I·S·T*. There was no sign of Buck or Herman at the *Quince* so they sat in the shadows and watched for the thieves.

Twenty minutes passed. Kate and Ginny came slowly down the hill beside Doud's Market. Ginny was watching the *Quince* while Kate had her eyes on the *M·I·S·T*. They got off their bikes and joined the boys aboard the yacht.

"Any action?" Kate asked.

"No," Dan said. "Nothing. Not even the family that chartered her."

"Don't you think it's time we turned in our badges?" Pete whispered.

"Please?" Eddie asked.

"You know, quit playing cops-and-robbers," Pete said. "How about we let all those state police and county sheriffs earn their keep?"

"Oh, Pete," Kate began, "there's no danger. We're just . . . "

"Kate," Pete said softly, "I was inches from taking

116

one of Herman's knives in the back—and not just once, twice. We *are* in danger. These guys are desperate. The best thing we can do is stay out of their way. If they want to board the *Quince* and sail off into the sunset—fine. I just don't think we need to be the ones to stop them."

"My dad called the mayor," Ginny said. "The mainland police will be coming on the next boat from Mackinaw City."

———

Thirty minutes later two uniformed men walked quickly along the marina dock toward the *M·I·S·T*. The five teens hopped off the Anderson yacht and met them.

"It was my father who called you," offered Ginny.

"All right," Sergeant Glenn said. "What's going on here?"

Dan stepped forward and explained all that had happened, from the warning message on Round Island to Pete's narrow escape from Herman's knives. He finished with a quick description of the two thieves.

The sergeant glanced at his deputy. "Did you get a look at those two men?—the ones that ran off the Arnold boat in Mackinaw City?" he asked.

"Not real close," the officer said with a shrug. "It could have been them. They sure were in a rush."

"Unfortunately," Sergeant Glenn said with a sigh, "nothing you've told us can be proven. Those initials, for example. They could refer to anyone—or anything. Those knives—who saw the man throw them?"

"I did!" Pete almost shouted. "One nicked my shoe and the other stuck in a tree next to my head. Couldn't have missed me by a foot."

"Anyone else see it?" the policeman asked. Everyone shook their heads.

"There, see?" Sergeant Glenn said. "Their word against just one boy's. There's nothing I can arrest a man

117

for. But, to be on the safe side, I'll keep Officer Beckman posted here at the sailboat. He'll talk to Mr. Meesley when he gets back. I'll spend a few days checking with those people whose initials you think were on that note. Now I'd like to see the barn where this Herman LeRoux is staying."

"Sure. It's up by Wawashkamo Golf Course," Dan said. "Follow us on our bikes."

Sergeant Glenn borrowed a dockmaster's two-wheeler and followed Pete and his friends up to the top of the island. They found all of Herman's trash, but the box was gone.

For the next two days, Officer Beckman guarded the yacht dock and Sergeant Glenn checked the other leads, but neither Buck nor Herman were nowhere to be found on Mackinac Island.

The *Quince*

CHAPTER 22
THE SWIM

Monday morning, two days later, Kate, Dan, Eddie and Pete lounged on the Andersons' spacious veranda, munching Danishes and sipping milk from crystal glasses. Fluffy, cumulus clouds drifted across the azure sky and a warm, gentle breeze wafted in from the Straits. Life for the four kids who were finishing their vacation on Mackinac Island had returned to normal.

Pete was content to watch the sailboats, cabin cruisers and freighters as they passed before him. Kate, Dan and Eddie on the other hand, were getting restless.

"It's a shame about that family that chartered the *Quince*," Eddie said. "Having their vacation cut short like that."

"Yeah, but it coulda been worse," Pete argued, "no telling what Buck Meesley mighta done to 'em. Imagine what a story those kids will have when they get home."

"I wonder what's become of Herman and Buck," Kate said, rocking in her oversized wicker chair.

"They're not on the Island," Eddie replied. "No cottages have been broken into for the last three days.

Ginny would have told us if they had."

Dan leaned forward in his chair and chose a juicy raspberry croissant from the silver platter. "Well, Aunt Nancy and Uncle George are happy that the police are staying until everything is cleared up."

"Yes, but they might be guarding an empty barn," Kate said. "I wouldn't be surprised if the horses aren't already out of the stable. You heard what Sergeant Glenn said when he met us at the yacht dock. Two men ran off the ferry in Mackinaw City as they were getting on. Buck and Herman could have taken Pete's bike down the hill and gotten aboard the Arnold boat even before we got to the marina."

"So, if they're not here, where are they?" Pete asked.

"South would be my guess," Eddie said. "Way south."

"Let's forget about them and go for a swim," Dan said.

"You mean at the Grand?" Pete asked. "No thanks. Last I checked, they were filling the pool with ice water."

"No," Dan said with a laugh. "We'll go to that shallow area on the lee side of Round Island. It's probably like bath water this time of the year."

"We'll take the *Griffin*," Eddie said. "I don't want any part of your uncle's dinghy. Not after our last trip. Besides, it wasn't nearly as rocky as I thought it would be. I saw several places we could beach her."

"What about the lighthouse keeper?" Pete asked. "What if he's still making his rounds like some people say?"

"That's ridiculous," Dan said. "Jesse Muldoon's been gone since the new light was built. All those stories of him guarding his island are nonsense. I'll bet he took his retirement check and is basking somewhere in the Bahamas."

"Ginny doesn't think so," Pete said. "She says people have seen someone walking that shore by the lighthouse."

"Ghost stories, most likely told around a campfire," Kate said. "No one's ever said for sure it was him."

"No, that's right. Not for sure," Pete agreed. "Okay, if you're all going, I'm not staying here by myself. I'll get my swim trunks."

"Great, we'll make a day of it," said Dan. "We'll get the picnic basket and ask Mrs. Odom to fill it up. Only this time we won't have any problems from Herman LeRoux."

"I'll call Ginny," Kate said. "I'm sure she'll want to come."

———

By ten A.M. the five friends had sailed the *Griffin* to the sheltered bay on the southeast side of Round Island. Eddie beached her on the sandy shore and the five were soon splashing in the warm shallows. By noon they had spread a picnic blanket and were munching their way through Mrs. Odom's basket of thick tuna salad sandwiches, fresh peaches and chocolate chip cookies.

"Let's walk to the lighthouse," Ginny suggested.

"Maybe you don't remember," said Pete, "but the last time we were there we were told not to come back."

"We all know it was Herman LeRoux that was behind that," Kate said. "And Herman is gone, right, Ginny?"

"That's right," Ginny replied. "Sergeant Glenn told my dad just this morning that two men who looked like Herman and Buck were nabbed in Illinois. They wouldn't admit it, but they couldn't give a good alibi, either. He was sure they'd get the truth out of them in a day or two. Besides, if they were still on the Island, someone would

121

have seen them by now. Mackinac isn't so big that two creeps like that could stay out of sight very long."

"Good enough for me," Dan said. "Let's get our shoes and go for a walk."

———

Half an hour later the five summer friends had hiked out on the long spit of land at the end of Round Island and up to the decaying lighthouse.

"Eddie, see if that door is still locked," Dan said.

Eddie twisted the handle. "It won't budge."

"Do you still have that key you found in Herman's box, Pete?" Kate asked.

"Yeah, it's right here," Pete said. "I kept it as a souvenir. Do you think it goes to this door?"

"Give it a try," Dan said.

Pete pulled the key from his pocket and slid it into the keyhole. He turned it and the door creaked open. The five stared at each other and then pushed their way inside, finding themselves in a large empty room.

"What are we waiting for?" Kate said, moving ahead. "Let's check it out."

"Are you sure you want to do this?" Pete said. "What if the old lighthouse keeper is hiding in one of the rooms?"

"Don't be silly," Kate said. "No one's been here since it was closed five years ago."

"I wonder how Herman got the key to this place," Eddie said.

"He might have stolen it from the Coast Guard station just like he was stealing from the cottages all summer," Kate said.

For the next twenty minutes the five adventurers wandered throughout the old building. They found the kitchen, the chart room, the office—even climbed to the tower. All were empty.

122

"It doesn't look like anyone's been here for a long time," Eddie said.

"So why did Herman have the key?" Pete asked.

"Oh, that lock is so simple, *any* old skeleton key could have opened it," Ginny said. "The one you used is probably for some other place."

"Hey, I've got an idea," Kate said. "Let's camp out here tonight." That `look' was in her eye. Pete, Dan and Eddie all recognized it.

Pete shook his head at the prospect. "Why would you want to do that?" he asked.

"Just because," Kate answered. "It would be fun."

"I don't think your aunt and uncle would let us." Pete persisted.

"Sure they would," said Kate. "Especially if Ginny came along. What do you say, Ginny?"

"I'm up for it. I'll have to ask my parents, but Dad always brags about his camping trips when he was a kid. So he can't really say no. Besides, it'll give me something different to write about in my column."

"This will be fun," Dan said. "We haven't camped out all summer."

"Uncle George has a bunch of pup tents he never uses," Kate added. "We'll pitch them here near the lighthouse."

"Great idea, Kate," Eddie said. "What do you say, Pete?"

"What if it rains?" Pete asked. "You know, a big storm comes along? It could blow us into the lake or something."

"That's what gave me the idea," Kate said. "With your key, we could just move inside. Oh, Pete, I'm so glad you found it."

Pete suddenly wished he had kept his souvenir a secret. "I'd feel a lot better if we knew for sure those guys in Illinois were really Buck and Herman," he said.

"It's got to be them," Ginny said. "Sergeant Glenn wouldn't have told my dad if he hadn't been certain."

Kate led the others out of the lighthouse and into the bright, early-afternoon sun. Pete took the skeleton key from his pocket and looked carefully at its simple design. He eyed the keyhole on the door. Ginny was right. This key probably could have unlocked half the doors in North America at one time. He slid it in, turned it and the bolt clicked back into place.

Pete caught up to the others, who were hurrying along the Round Island shore chattering about the night's plans. Camping out, all five of them together, would be a great way to finish their stay at Mackinac.

Skull Cave

CHAPTER 23
THE PLAN

As Buck and Herman stole silently through the woods from Skull Cave that night, Buck recalled the storm last November when he changed the course of his fishing boat—and the direction of his life forever.

Buck had known then that when the *Irish Eyes* didn't return to port within the next few days, the people of Little Perch Bay would think that he and his mates had gone down in the storm. For most of the townspeople, the period of mourning would be very brief. Only the banker cared whether Buck returned—and then only so he could foreclose on his loan. Oh, *he'd* be crying, all right.

Buck remembered that the Cheboygan harbor had lots of old merchant schooners rotting away in dry dock. He figured he could trade the *Irish Eyes* for one of them, fit it out as a pleasure boat and start a chartering service for wealthy, downstate people on summer vacations. But that would just be a front for a bigger plan.

"By next fall, we're gonna be richer than that banker and all the fishermen in Little Perch Bay put

125

together," Buck said.

"And just how you plannin' on doin' that?" Sam asked. "There ain't much money in the charter business. Besides, you won't get Herman an' me on no joy boat. You might be able to kowtow to them high-falutin', rich folks, but that ain't for me and Herman."

"That's right," Buck said, "but I got plans for both of you. Sam, I know you want to be on the water. Them ore boats are always lookin' for deck hands. I'm gonna need you aboard one of 'em—but not just any one. It's gotta be a freighter that cuts between Mackinac and Round Island on a regular basis. Them Tartan Steel boats go by every week. One of 'em would do us just fine."

"What about me?" Herman said. "I've had it bein' on the Lakes. I ain't workin' no fancy blow boat, an' I sure ain't crewin' aboard no stinkin' freighter."

"No boats, Herman," Buck said. "Your job'll be what you' always been good at. You know how you can always get yourself in and out of places without bein' caught, eh? You broke into Rosa's Grocery anytime we needed some grub and got out without ol' Earl ever suspectin' it. You was the one that got us into Doc Grimson's house and made that fire look all accidental. I bet you could sneak into those ritzy cottages on Mackinac, swipe a few knickknacks from each one and get out without no one the wiser for it. How's that sound?"

Herman thought for a moment. "Yeah," Herman said, "I'd like that, all right." Then he nodded in the direction of the bay ahead of him and the large summer homes along the Cheboygan shoreline. "But why Mackinac? Why not here?"

"The `Why' is 'cause we gotta get the stuff you heist to Sam without drawin' suspicion to him or me. An' I'm gonna be workin' real legal-like out of Cheboygan. Besides there's more big houses on Mackinac than here.

126

I'll snoop aroun' there every now and then and get you a list of the best ones. I'll even make a map for ya an' tell ya when to go into 'em."

"An' what's my part in this?" Sam asked.

"We'll get your freighter schedule," Buck nodded to his tall friend, "and when you go past Mackinac, Herman'll put the stuff he's ripped off in a bag, eh? He'll tie it to a buoy and drop it off so's you can pick it up with a pike pole or somethin'. You'll take it down to Chicago and fence it for cash. When you come back north, you'll drop the money in a float an' Herman'll pick it up. When the summer's over we'll go south to Jamaica or somewheres and live like kings."

The three stared at the Cheboygan harbor as the *Irish Eyes* plowed into port. The rain stopped and five minutes later a brilliant saffron sky broke through the clouds in the west.

Sam Moilanen stood shuddering wet and cold in the November afternoon. "All right, Buck, I'm in," he finally said. "I got nothin' to lose."

A snaggletoothed grin slowly formed on Herman's lips. "Me, too," he said. "Just so long as I don' hafta be on no more boats. I kinda like the idea of lightenin' the loads of rich folks. I bet I could be real good at it."

As the three men looked ahead, a smirk crept across each of their faces. It would be just like the old days when they skipped school and did all the things Buck told them to do.

Yes, those were the good ol' days.

The Anderson Cottage - Backdoor

CHAPTER 24
THE LAST JOB

In the fading light, Buck and Herman sneaked along the back road behind the West Bluff summer homes.

"I'll be glad to get off'n this here rock," Herman said. "That cave was gettin' on my nerves. Especially with all them bats flyin' roun'."

"Well, tonight's the night," Buck said. "Sam's boat comes through at 3:30, down bound and heavy. He better remember that emergency signal I told him about when we was makin' our plans. If he ain't ready with a boardin' ladder to pull us up instead of just a hook to haul in the buoy, we'll be done for."

"Don't be talkin' like that, Buck," Herman said. "He'll be ready."

"You got that key on ya?" Buck asked.

"To the lighthouse? Yeah, right here," Herman answered. He flipped open the latch of his old tackle box and sifted past the envelope of money, Buck's list of jobs, several knives and the boat schedule. He felt around in the bottom. "It ain't here!" Herman said. "It musta fallen outta my pocket in the loft."

"Well, we ain't lookin' for it now," Buck said. "We'll just bash in the lighthouse door when we get there. All we have to do is run up to the tower, give Sam the signal, watch for his answer and then row out to the freighter. After we're aboard the *V.A. Frazier* I don't care what happens to the lighthouse. No one would ever look for us on no ore boat. But now we've got one last job here on Mackinac."

"The big house on the West Bluff, eh?"

"Just the gold and jewels," Buck said, nodding. "And from what I hear, that's all we'll ever need again."

It was 7:30 and the sun was setting as the burglars skulked through the woods, shouldering their two gunnysacks. As they crept along, they escaped the attention of all but the Andersons' horses. Buck and Herman smelled so bad after their stay in Skull Cave that one persnickety Arabian mare began to snort loudly at the foul odor. Soon, when the two men got downwind from the barn, the temperamental riding horse quit her noisy protests.

Through the shadows, Buck and Herman watched Mr. and Mrs. Anderson step grandly from the front veranda, walk down the long stairway and enter a hansom carriage for a night on the town.

The thieves' only obstacle was to get into the back door, past the woman who seemed to live in the kitchen and up the wide staircase to the master bedroom.

By 9:30, darkness had closed in over Mackinac Island. The old summer mansion was cast in dim shadows and most of the servants' lights were out. Buck nodded to Herman to begin their job. Herman shook his head. "Too soon," he said. "A kitchen light is still on. The butler and the cook are in there. Ten minutes and it'll be okay."

For once Buck listened to Herman. Buck was in the habit of telling Herman what to do, but this time he deferred to the experience of his wily partner who, over the past three months, had gained entry to dozens of homes without being caught. Herman motioned to Buck to stay where he was, then crept nearer to the back door.

From within, he heard a man with a British accent ask, "Where are Master Daniel, Miss Kate and their two houseguests?"

"They gone off campin' fer the night," a woman answered with a Southern drawl. "I don't 'spect they' be back 'til morn'n—an' late at that—tired an' hungry, I should guess. My, how they love t' play their games. But no more'n Master George did when he was a pup. Lan' sakes, I could tell stories 'bout him as a boy."

"I'm sure you could, Mrs. Odom," the butler said. "Well, it'll be a long day tomorrow. I'd better get to bed. Good night, Mrs. Odom.

"Y'sir, Mister Charles," the cook said. "I' be turnin' in m'self now. G'night."

Herman heard some shuffling of chairs, then footsteps leading to the servants' quarters. In ten minutes, all was quiet in the old mansion.

He nodded to Buck, who remained crouched in the shadows behind a lilac bush. They crept softly up the back steps. A breeze came over the trees, blowing past them toward the horse barn. A loud whinny came from the stable. The Arabian mare had caught their scent. Instantly, Herman spun on his heels, crouched low and snatched a dagger from his leg scabbard. He cocked the knife behind his ear, ready to flick it into the chest of any unfortunate intruder. Buck knelt beside him on the darkened back porch, his eyes darting into the empty night.

The air grew still. A minute passed. False alarm.

131

Herman returned the blade to its sheath and grasped the doorknob. He pushed it open and stepped into the kitchen. An electric clock above the stove provided just enough light for him to slip down the hallway to the dining room. Buck followed, his taller, whiter frame standing out in the shadows. They moved into the spacious living room. Moonlight poured through the blue, leaded-glass windows, making it easy for them to find the main stairway. The two thieves climbed the glistening hardwood steps, ever closer to their bounty of riches.

They inched along the second-floor hallway, stopping at a narrow door. "This might be it," Herman whispered to Buck.

"This might be what?" Buck growled.

"Most of these joints have hidden storage rooms," Herman said, "secret vaults for jewels and stuff." Herman drew the door open. He felt around on the walls of the linen closet, probing high and low for a lever that would disclose a false door. Finally, he shook his head. "It ain't here," he said. "They must keep everything in the big bedroom."

Herman motioned for Buck to stay close and they walked into the master bedchamber. Everywhere they turned were gold necklaces, diamond bracelets and emerald brooches, gleaming in the moonlit room. A half-dozen jewelry boxes lined the dressers, each fuller than the last with costly gems.

Herman stood transfixed. Buck stared at the splendor of the room's wealth. He didn't know where to begin. Each object seemed to pale in comparison with the magnificence of the next. "I don't know," he said, guessing Herman's thoughts. "Just grab the heaviest stuff you can carry and hope we can get out of here without the stairs collapsin'."

In each hand they snatched jewel after jewel,

132

cramming them into their gunnysacks. When the bags were full, they eased their way out of the bedroom into the hallway. With each step the old planks groaned under the weight of the glorious plunder.

Buck guessed he was hauling a good million dollars in gold, diamonds and emeralds. Herman, too, must have an equal amount of loot.

Now all that remained was to row out to Round Island and climb aboard the *V.A. Frazier*—and begin their new life of luxury.

Campfire - Strange Tales Told

CHAPTER 25
CAMP OUT

"That was easier than I thought it would be," Eddie said as the five pulled up to the bicycle stand at the yacht dock. "We didn't even have to make up a story about where we were going."

Kate looked at Ginny. "Aunt Nancy would never have agreed to this if you hadn't been able to come," she said.

"My mom wasn't keen on the whole idea either," Ginny said, "but Dad thought, as long as you were going, it would be all right. Besides, I think he expects it'll make a good article for my next `Kids Kolumn'."

"Let's get aboard before they change their minds," Eddie said.

In minutes the three boys and two girls had the tents, sleeping bags and food stowed away in the twenty-five-foot sloop. Soon the *Griffin* was rigged and Eddie was guiding her out of the harbor. As they approached Round Island, Eddie leaned over the side to check the depth of the water.

"I think we can beach her near the lighthouse," Eddie said. "That would save us a long hike from where we landed this morning."

"I'm for that," Kate said.

"Pete, crawl out on the bow and watch for boulders," Eddie directed. "Dan, be ready to raise the centerboard. Kate, on my signal you can drop the jib. We'll take her in real slow."

A minute later the *Griffin* came to a halt on the pebbly shore. The five campers hopped out and pulled the sailboat a few feet onto the beach.

"Let's pitch our tents now," Kate suggested. "I don't want to wait till dark to set them up. Last time I camped out, I ended up with my sleeping bag on a nest of fire ants. They bit like little piranhas. I itched for a week. This time I want to make sure what I'm sleeping on."

"I remember that trip," Dan said. "That same night I layed my bedroll on top of a rock. I couldn't walk straight for three days."

After our tents are up," Eddie said, "lets find some kindling and start a fire."

"It was a good idea to camp near the lighthouse," Dan said. "As clear as the sky looks now, I'd hate to get stuck in a rainstorm with these little pup tents."

Ginny looked toward St. Ignace. "I hadn't noticed it before, but there are some mean-looking clouds off to the west. Pete, you brought your souvenir, right?"

"Huh? Oh, yeah," Pete said. He pulled the skeleton key from his pocket. "Right here."

"Let's scrounge up some firewood," Dan said. "Kate, you and Ginny can gather tinder along the shore while Pete, Eddie and I go into the woods and find some dry logs."

"We'll meet back here in half an hour and start the fire," Kate said. "By then, we'll probably all be hungry."

———

They cooked their dinner over a bed of red-hot

136

coals. Everyone feasted on the steaks, corn-on-the-cob
and tossed green salad that Mrs. Odom had packed in the
wicker basket.

The sun was approaching the western rim as the
explorers sat around the crackling embers. They took
turns roasting marshmallows with forked branches Pete
had cut with his jackknife. They faced the fire, their backs
shadowing the openings to each of their own pup tents,
assured that they would be sleeping over nothing but soft,
bug-free sand.

By eight o'clock the sun had set and a few stars
could be seen in the east. Along the western horizon an
amazing display of purples, yellows and reds, especially
on the edges of a few billowing clouds, dazzled the
campers' eyes. Soon the heavens darkened and stars
began to burst forth like popcorn on a hot iron skillet.

By nine o'clock the fire was dying into a small pile
of glowing coals and a late-August night chill was settling
over the peaceful scene.

"Do you think your key might work on that
outhouse, Pete?" Eddie asked, nodding to a small
brick structure.

"I was just wondering the same thing," Pete
replied. He took the key from his pocket and walked to
the nearby building. "Presto," he said as the latch creaked
open. Immediately, three bats darted out over his head,
chirping into the night air. Pete jumped back and waited
to make certain there were no more surprises. "Who
wants to be first?" he said nervously.

"I'm not afraid of bats," Eddie said. He walked
boldly toward the opening, but then stopped and peeked
timidly inside before entering. After Eddie took his turn,
in went Ginny, then Kate, followed shortly by Dan and
Pete. Soon all returned to their places around the fire.

The starlit sky was now in full bloom, the

traditional time for campers to tell their best stories.

Ginny began with a tale about a sailing ship in 1832 that wasn't allowed to land at Mackinac Harbor. Some of its passengers were sick and fear of a cholera plague steeled the hearts of the Islanders against the seafaring strangers.

"The captain had to anchor here off Round Island," she said. "He brought the passengers ashore in a dory. They had to stay in quarantine for two weeks. As the days passed, one by one, each of the travellers, devoured by fever and racked in pain, screamed to a horrible death. The brave captain suffered the worst and was the last to die. Two weeks later soldiers came from the fort and found the captain's decayed body sprawled here on this very part of the beach. His bony arms were stretched toward Mackinac and his mouth was wide-open, frozen for all eternity in his last pitiful scream of death.

"Sometimes, when I'm at home in bed, I'll be startled by bloodcurdling wails coming from across the water. I'll sit up, scared out of my wits and listen. At first, I'll think it's a dream, but then, as I'm sitting silently, barely breathing, my eyes wide open, I hear it again. The first time it happened I was three, maybe four years old. I pulled off my covers and ran to my parents' room. I asked my father what the horrible sound was. I'll never forget his answer. `Ginny,' he said, `some people think it's sea gulls fighting over the carcass of a fish—a trout or a pike, risen from the deep in death. The cry is, indeed, a fair likeness. But those who know of that ancient cholera ship—they'll tell you what it really is. For in truth, it is the captain's ghost, pacing Round Island's shore throughout eternity, mournfully calling for the merciful rescue of his passengers—a plea that will never be answered."

As the others sat in terrified silence, Ginny gazed

138

in the direction of the lighthouse. The red glow of the campfire played in the shadows of her face. Her eyes grew wide. The others stared as her jaw suddenly dropped. Terror overtook Ginny's face and she jumped to her feet, pointed and shrieked, "There he is!"

Her four friends leaped from the sand, nearly snapping their necks as they turned to see where Ginny was pointing. They stared into the pitch-black night, neither seeing nor hearing even the faintest sign of the phantom. Several moments went by and each of the listeners turned to see again where Ginny was facing.

When she had their undivided attention, her expression changed. She burst into laughter. "That's the best ever," she gasped, tears streaming down her cheeks. "I've told that story a dozen times and never got anyone as good as I got you guys."

One by one, they all sat back down, their hearts still beating wildly, but relieved that they had simply been duped by a clever storyteller and not haunted by an ancient mariner.

Next, it was Dan's turn. "This isn't really a story," he began, matter-of-factly. "It's just something that happened at our cottage one time. We had just finished dinner. No dessert had been prepared, so our chef, Mr. Argo, said he'd go to the boathouse and get some ice cream from the freezer chest. I wanted to stretch my legs, so I went along. Mr. Argo lifted the freezer door and there inside, frozen stiff, was our cat, Trixie. `Dan!' the chef called. `Give me a hand! Trixie must have jumped in here when I got the frozen peas before dinner.' We reached in and gently set Trixie on the floor. Then Mr. Argo hurried over to a gas can and poured a drop on his finger. He touched it to the cat's tongue and immediately, Trixie jumped up, ran around in circles and then fell down, right at my feet."

Everyone stared blankly at Dan.

Finally, Pete, wide-eyed, whispered, "Was she dead?"

"No," Dan said slowly, with his unmistakable southern Ohio drawl, "she just ran out of gas."

The other listeners, including Ginny, all having heard Dan's favorite story before, rolled hysterically in the sand. Pete, on the other hand, could do nothing but sit there, his face growing warm and shake his head. He was so glad to know that he could bring such joy so simply to this conniving pack of so-called friends.

Eddie finally got up and added two small logs to the fire while the others regained their breath and wiped the sand from their tear-streaked faces.

Next, Ginny told another story about an English commander at Fort Mackinac. "Way back in 1795," she said, "when Captain Daniel Robertson was in charge of Fort Mackinac, he went hunting with a bunch of his officers on a nearby island. It happened to be the same island where a tribe of Ojibwas were camping. There, by chance, he met a beautiful Indian princess. They fell in love at first sight, but unknown to Captain Robertson, the princess was already spoken for. She was supposed to marry a chief from a distant tribe who was many years older than she and who already had four wives. She was sickened by his ugliness and despised him, but her father, who was the chief of her tribe, insisted that she marry him.

"She begged Captain Robertson to take her to Mackinac Island and marry her and so he did. On their wedding night, they had a huge reception at his new home on the edge of the bluff. With the party in full swing, the ugly chief came to take her away. He grabbed her and in the scuffle, they both fell over the cliff, landing two hundred feet below on the rocky shore. They both were dead."

Ginny pointed toward Mackinac Island's East Bluff. "Right there," she said. "That's where it happened." Her four listeners shuddered, looking across the water to the twinkling lights on Mackinac Island's now peaceful eastern shore.

Between stories, the boys put small pieces of driftwood on the crackling coals. The branches leapt into brilliant flames as the hungry embers feasted on the dry offerings. In minutes the twigs were reduced to glowing remnants.

"We'd better be sure this fire is dead out before we turn in," Dan said. "Remember how parched the golf course was? It would take only one flying spark and by morning this whole island—us included—would be nothing more than a charred pile of ashes."

Another hour passed. Ginny had fallen asleep with her head resting on a *Griffin* boat cushion. Kate, also exhausted, tapped Ginny on the shoulder and the two went into their tents. Dan, Eddie and Pete poured handfuls of water over the glowing coals until the embers no longer hissed and no steam clouds rose from the blackened logs.

Before long the campers were fast asleep. A soft rain began to fall. It was only a gentle sprinkle at first, but by two A.M. a storm was coming in earnest.

Buck And Herman Crossing Round Island

CHAPTER 26
THE TOWER

Back on Mackinac Island, by one A.M., Buck
Meesley and Herman LeRoux had hauled their gunnysacks
crammed with gold, silver and jewels down the hill
through a soft rain to Biddle Point.

"Get a move on," Buck snarled. "This ain't no
walk in the park. Where's that rowboat?"

"Not far," Herman answered. "Look, I gotta take a
break. I can't carry this no more."

"You *can* and you *will*," Buck snapped. "If we
stop now, we might miss Sam's freighter. Keep movin' or
I'll bust your stubby little legs and leave you here to rot."

"No need to get all riled," Herman panted. "The
boat's just ahead." They walked another fifty yards along
the shore to a clump of lilac bushes. "There she is. Help
me flip her over."

They righted the boat, dragged it across the pebbly
beach and eased it into the Straits water. They loaded
their heavy cargo in the bow and Buck stepped aboard,
taking his place in the middle and setting the oars in their
locks. Herman pushed off, then seated himself in the stern
facing forward.

143

"Keep me on a dead line for the lighthouse," Buck said. "We can't waste no time gettin' over there."

"Gotcha, Buck," Herman said. "Just follow my hand. That storm to the west is comin' fast. There's lightnin' off by St. Ignace."

"Pete!" Dan said. "Wake up!"

"Huh?" Pete mumbled. "Where are we?"

"It's raining hard," Dan said. "Come on. These pup tents won't last. The wind is picking up and they'll be blown into the lake before we know it."

"Yeah, okay," Pete muttered. "I'll be along in a few minutes."

"No!" Dan yelled. "Now! The others are already at the lighthouse! Hurry!"

Pete burrowed himself deeper into his sleeping bag. It was every bit as comfortable as any bed he had ever slept on. "I don't hear any wind," he mumbled.

"It's coming," Dan said. "We're in for a bad storm."

Pete sighed, opened the knapsack and rolled to his feet.

"Come on," Dan said. "Where's your key?"

"In my pocket," Pete said. He stepped out of his tent and felt the wind and rain on his face. Along the western horizon he saw great bolts of lightning dancing across the sky and heard the low rumble of thunder in the distance.

"Grab your sleeping bag," Dan said.

Pete followed Dan to the lighthouse, where at the door stood Eddie, Kate and Ginny wrapped in their bedrolls.

"How could you have been *so* asleep?" Kate asked. "Hurry! Let us in!"

Pete turned the skeleton key in the hole. With the

144

next gust, the door flew open and everyone rushed inside. Pete tried to close the door, but with the wind, he couldn't force it shut. Eddie joined Pete and together the two leaned against the door. Finally it closed.

"Better lock it, Pete," Dan said. "If it isn't latched tight, it'll fly open and break itself to pieces by morning."

"We can't stay here," Kate said. "If the water rises, it'll flood the floor."

"We'll go to the tower," Dan said, aiming his flashlight toward the stairway. "Follow me."

Everyone moved to the circular staircase and headed high into the tower. They spread their sleeping bags on the lamp room floor and with the calming drone of the rain on the thick lighthouse windows, all were soon fast asleep.

———

"Ease up on them oars," Herman said. "We're almost there. With all this weight, we don't wanna punch no hole in the bottom." The wooden hull scraped along the shore. "What time you got?"

As rain poured down in torrents, Buck clicked the flashlight and brought it close to his wrist. "Three o'clock," he said. "We got thirty minutes. Grab a side and help me haul her up. We'll go to the tower and watch for Sam. C'mon, move it! I'm gettin' soaked."

A brilliant flash struck a nearby tree, followed instantly by a deafening blast of thunder.

"That was close," Buck said. "The storm'll be passin' soon. We'll leave the sacks here. No sense haulin' 'em inside."

The two raced to the lighthouse door. Buck tried the knob but it was locked. He stepped back, gave a savage kick and snapped the dead bolt with his heel. The door flew open and struck the wall with a crash. As the gale screamed through the Straits, the door slammed back

145

and forth on its hinges.

———

"What was *that*?" Dan startled, sitting up in his
sleeping bag.

"Just thunder," reassured Eddie. "Go back
to sleep."

"Listen close, Eddie, that's not thunder," Dan said.
"Pete! Wake up!"

"Huh?" Pete said, once again shaking the cobwebs
from his head.

"Didn't you lock the door after we came in,"
Dan said.

"Yeah," Pete replied.

"Then it shouldn't be banging like it is," Dan said.
"Hear that?"

Below them Pete heard something crashing against
a wall—a window shutter perhaps, or a door flapping in
the stiff breeze.

"Are you *sure* you locked it?" Dan asked.

"Not anymore," Pete said. He got out of his warm
sleeping bag and stood up. The nearly continuous
lightning, lit his way to the handrail that led from the
tower room to the lower levels of the building.

"Do you want the flashlight?" Eddie asked.

"I won't need it," Pete said groggily. "I'll be right
back." Pete started down the long staircase and soon
wished he had taken Eddie up on his offer. Boy was it
dark! Feeling his way along the railing, Pete had almost
reached the bottom when he heard voices ahead of him.
Who could that be? he wondered. *Maybe they're boaters
who ran aground in the storm and came here for shelter.
They might need some help.* Pete moved down the last
few steps. Lightning outside the open door revealed the
shapes of two men standing in front of him no more than
thirty feet away.

146

"Gimme that flashlight," one snapped at the other. "I can't see nothin' in here."

Pete heard a click and a narrow ray of light illuminated the room. The larger man aimed the light at the circular stairway leading to the lighthouse tower where Pete stood.

He was just about to step forward and offer his assistance when instead, he shrank back into the shadows. Something about their voices made him leery. As the light swept closer, he forced himself into a narrow closet.

Pete stood still, scarcely breathing. He heard footsteps and the voices grew louder. The men were coming toward him.

As they approached, one of them said, "I hope this blasted rain lets up by the time the *V.A. Frazier* gets here."

The *V.A. Frazier*? Pete thought. *That's how I know that voice! It's Buck Meesley!*

"I sure hope Sam remembers the signal," the other said.

That's Herman! Pete realized. The memory of a knife whizzing past his left ear and slamming into a tree trunk nearly drained the blood from his head. Pete grew weak in the knees, realizing his desperate situation—and that of his friends in the tower. Pete leaned against the wall, steadying himself.

"Sam knows it, all right," Buck said with a low growl. "And he better be ready to haul us and the loot we got in the rowboat. If he don't, I'll snap his scrawny little neck."

Pete's head was spinning. *They're going to the tower? They'll find Kate and everyone up there for sure. But what can I do? If I try to stop them, they'll grab me and still find the others. Our only chance is for me to get out of here.*

The two thugs followed the long stairway high into

147

the lighthouse. They reached the top and as Buck entered the lamp room, he nearly tripped on a sleeping bag. He stepped back in surprise and then aimed his flashlight into Kate's eyes.

"What's this?" he bellowed.

At once, Kate, Dan, Eddie and Ginny sat up, blinded by the beam's brilliance.

"Don't none of you move," Buck shouted.

"It's those kids we seen at the barn!" Herman said. "What're we gonna do, Buck?"

"Shut up, Herman, I'm thinkin'," Buck snarled. "I know this much. We can't let 'em outta here alive. An' whatever we do, we gotta make it look like an accident."

Herman glanced outside toward the shipping channel. "Sam's coming," he yelled. "I can see the *Frazier's* bow light. She's maybe five miles away. She'll be here in fifteen minutes tops."

"I got it!" Buck said. "You tie these brats up while I signal Sam. When he answers we'll start a little housewarming party like we done for ol' Doc Grimson."

"That'll work," Herman smiled. "It'll look like they broke into the lighthouse, got cold and lit a fire. Then the blaze went outta control and they got themselves trapped up here in the tower. By tomorrow mornin' there'll be nothin' left of them or the lighthouse but smoke and ashes."

"And we'll be bound for Chicago, safe and rich," Buck added. "All right, you little creeps, outta them sleepin' bags—one at a time. You first, Blondie."

Kate stepped from her bedroll and stood defiantly before the two men. Herman drew a dagger from his leg scabbard and pressed the cold blade hard against her wildly pulsating throat. He leered at her, his rotting teeth and dreadful breath inches from her face, then pulled the knife away and sliced the drawstring from her sleeping

148

bag. He ran the cord several times around her wrists and snubbed it tightly before knotting the ends. He shoved her to the floor and tied her feet to her hands. Kate winced but didn't cry out. She wasn't going to give him the satisfaction of knowing that he had hurt her.

Herman continued around the room with the others and was just starting to tie Eddie's wrists when Buck, who had been shining his flashlight toward the oncoming ore boat, turned to Herman. "That's it," Buck said. "Sam got the message. We got ten minutes to get out there. Finish up what you gotta do here—you know what I mean—an' be quick about it."

"Grab a couple of them sleepin' bags, Buck," Herman said, staring at the four terrified captives. He rubbed his thumb across the dagger blade. "I'll need 'em to start the fire. Better bust up some of them cabinets down there, too. We'll need plenty of kindlin'."

Buck scooped up three bedrolls and turned to the door. "Don't be wastin' no time playin' with 'em," he said over his shoulder as he disappeared down the stairs.

Robber's Loot

CHAPTER 27
PETE'S PLAN

Pete dashed out of the lighthouse into the night.
The storm had passed and the overcast blackness had given
way to a starlit sky. He moved quickly along the shore.
A brilliant quarter moon darted in and out from behind the
last of the storm's remaining clouds. In the distance he saw
the *Griffin* and the five tents. Nearer, something was on
the beach that he couldn't identify. The moon again burst
from its cover and Pete could see clearly that the object
was a small outboard.

Pete remembered Buck's words, "—*the loot we got
in the rowboat*—" and, like the lightning bolts that had lit
up the sky, a plan flashed into his head. He ran to the
thieves' dory, grabbed the sacks and lugged them to his
tent. He opened the bags and dumped the precious
contents onto the ground inside, he then closed the flap
and turned away.

He hurried back to the rowboat, filled the sacks
with rocks and set them in the bow where he had found
them. Next, he returned to the lighthouse. As he crept
along the outside he saw a radiant glow flickering inside
the building.

He stepped around the corner and peeked through
the open door. Herman LeRoux was wrapping a sleeping
bag around the smoldering base of the building's main
support pillar. Across the room, Buck Meesley was
breaking up a cabinet and throwing the pieces of wood
onto the fire. Pete's blood froze.

"Buck!" Herman yelled, "how come we got five

sleepin' bags here?"

"Five?" Buck shouted, turning toward Herman. "You sure?"

"Look for yourself, eh?" Herman said. "There's the ones you brung down, three of 'em and here's the two I got."

"Hey! Wasn't there *five* kids that day at the barn?" Buck yelled.

"Yeah and the one that's not up in the tower is that skinny runt that dodged my knives. He's gotta be around here somewhere," Herman snarled. "He's the same one that jumped me from the loft. I got my own score to settle with *him*."

"We ain't got no time!" Buck yelled. "Get that fire goin'. The *Frazier* will be passin' through in five minutes."

"We can't just leave him here alive," Herman argued. "He knows too much."

"You're right," Buck said as he dumped an armload of kindling in the doorway. "Two minutes. That's all we got. I'll search inside. You check outside. Hurry!"

Herman threw the sleeping bags onto the blaze, grabbed his flashlight and ran out the door. He aimed the search beam in all directions. The woods looked to be too far away, so Herman reasoned Pete couldn't have gotten *that* far. Herman concentrated on the other nearby hiding places. He caught sight of the outhouse. He ran to it, kicked in the door and checked high and low. It was empty.

He shone his light in a full circle around him. Just beyond his dory, he saw a beached sailboat silhouetted in the moonlight. He ran toward it, noting several small tents along the way. He boarded the *Griffin* and bashed in the cabin door. He aimed his light into the tiny compartment. No one was there. He jumped off and raced to the first tent. Nothing. He checked the second, the third and the fourth—all were empty.

As he reached for the flap of the last one, Buck yelled, "We gotta go. She's comin'!"

Herman glanced at the lighthouse. He saw the fire raging in the doorway and Buck sprinting toward the rowboat. He looked into the channel. He *felt*, as much as saw, the *V.A. Frazier* pounding toward them only two minutes away.

He turned to the sprinting Buck. "He ain't out here!" Herman yelled as he raced to meet his partner.

"I couldn't find him, either," Buck shouted. "There's a dozen rooms in there where he could be hidin', but I got a blaze goin' real good at the door. If he's inside, he'll never make it out. In a few minutes the lighthouse will cave in and he'll be burnt to a crisp along with his little friends."

The two shoved the rowboat out onto the water and jumped aboard. Buck sat in the middle and pulled the oars directly towards the oncoming, five-hundred-foot freighter.

Herman flashed a signal and from the ship's stern came a reply. Buck rowed with all his might as the *V.A. Frazier* thundered into the narrow pass. The huge vessel pushed a wall of water ahead of its bow and the rowboat rose high on the wave. Still, Buck pulled on the oars until his tiny boat was along the port side of the immense ship.

Over the low-pitched drone of the V.A. Frazier's engine, Buck yelled, "Grab a sack and latch onto the ladder!"

"I'm right behind you," Herman answered.

Herman reached for the bottom rung and kicked the rowboat away. Above, on the stern deck, Sam Moilanen cranked the ladder bringing his two partners aboard like lake trout in a gill net—only these fish carried a treasure that would make them rich forever.

153

Boarding The *Frazier*

CHAPTER 28
THE INFERNO

Buck and Herman are going out to the freighter, Pete thought. *Now's my chance to save Kate and the others. I hope it's not too late.* He ran to the lighthouse and saw the doorway engulfed in a wall of flames. Through the smoky heat, he could see the blaze raging at the base of the lighthouse's main support pillar. *I have to stop that fire or the whole place will collapse before I can reach the top! I've got to get through this door.*

Pete ran to the lake and jumped in. He pulled off his T-shirt and tied it around his head, covering his mouth. Shivering and soaking wet, he raced back to the lighthouse. Ten feet from the flaming door he took a deep breath, measured his steps and leaped through the wall of fire.

He dashed to the wooden beam and tried to pull the blazing sleeping bags away from the base, but the white-hot material scorched his hands. He kicked at it with his feet but the flames snapped hungrily at his bare legs. His eyelashes began to crinkle and his eyeballs burned as if branded by a poker. Frantically, while he could still see, he glanced around the floor, into the corners, high and low, for a pail, a can—anything he could use to carry water to douse the flames.

Poisonous fumes filled the room and Pete began to cough. The blistering heat seared his lungs. In moments he was too weak to stand and he slumped to his knees. Steam poured from his soaked clothes. *I can't breathe*, Pete realized. *I'm burning up! I'll never make it out of here!*

He swayed for a moment, then pitched forward, falling face-first onto the stone floor. He lay there gasping, consciousness draining swiftly from his parched body. He closed his eyes. A sense of calm came over him. Slowly, the tremendous roar of the blaze diminished to a faint whisper. *Good*, Pete thought, *the fire's burning itself out. If I lie here quietly, I'll be okay.*

The room became silent. In the distance, Pete heard footsteps approaching. *Finally!* Pete thought. *The fire is dead. Someone has come to save us.*

"Gimme a hand!" a gruff voice demanded.

Who could that be? Pete wondered. He opened his eyes and squinted, trying to see through the dense smoke. To his surprise, the fire was still raging and its roar instantly thundered back into his ears. Still, there was someone moving toward him. Someone hauling two large wooden buckets.

"Wh-who are you?" Pete blurted out.

"Never mind that," the man said. He dumped a pail of water onto Pete's head. A strange sense of warmth flowed over him. The man unloaded the second bucket on Pete's back and legs. "Get up! I got two more pails by the boat launch. This old lighthouse ain't goin' up in flames as long as I'm still around."

Pete blinked, not really believing what he saw, yet knowing immediately who the scrawny old man in the dark uniform had to be. "Are you Jesse Muldoon?—the lighthouse keeper?" he asked as he pulled himself to his feet.

"I was till they built that dad-gum, newfangled one across the way," the old man growled. "Now, get a move on. I can't put this fire out b' m'se'f."

Mr. Muldoon turned and strode toward the far wall. Pete followed as the old keeper stepped through a narrow doorway. Pete glanced at his new surroundings and realized that he was in some sort of boathouse area. The smoke here wasn't nearly as thick and Pete could see his rescuer clearly. Jesse Muldoon wore a full lighthouse keeper's uniform, boots and master's cap. The bright brass buttons on his coat reflected the fire raging in the other room. Jesse shoved two buckets toward the gawking Pete Jenkins.

"Fill 'em up and follow me," the man said and he scooped his pails full of lake water.

Pete did as he was told and hurried behind the old man to the main room. The air here was worse than before but Jesse Muldoon walked straight for the central column, seemingly unaffected by the heat and smoke. He emptied his pails on the sleeping bags, but the fire continued to rage until Pete dumped the water from his pails and great plumes of steam issued from the blaze. The flames sputtered and went out.

Pete glanced at the lighthouse entrance where the other fire was advancing up the wall to the ceiling.

He looked back and saw Jesse Muldoon disappear through the boathouse door. Pete ran to his side. Again both filled their pails and returned to the main room. This time the old man marched to the front doorway and dumped one bucket on the left side and the second one on the right. Pete followed the old man's example, dousing each side of the door. Again, billows of steam replaced the flames, leaving the entrance charred but the fire

157

smoldering for only a few moments before going out.

Pete spun around to look for the old man, but he had vanished.

At once, Pete remembered his four friends. A wave of horror swept over him as he imagined them lying in pools of their own blood, their necks slashed by Herman's razor-sharp daggers. *I've got to hurry*, he thought. *Please, let them be alive.*

Through the smoky darkness, Pete raced up the stairs. What had seemed so short a distance before, now felt like miles to his aching legs.

Finally, he burst into the lamp room. It was as dark and silent as a coalminer's grave. He stared for several moments at the floor. He was too exhausted to call out his friends' names and afraid that, even if he could, there would be no response. He listened intently for some sign of life, some hint that his companions had been spared. But he heard nothing. He knew at that instant that they all were dead.

Hateful thoughts for the two killers filled his head as tears of loss for his summer friends flooded his heart. Overcome with emotion, Pete turned and stumbled toward the stairway. A low, mournful groan seeped from his soul.

From behind him something rustled on the cold, stone floor.

Pete spun on his heels. "K-Kate?" he whispered.

"Who's there?" Kate called out. "Is that you, Pete?"

"Yeah, it's me! Are you okay?"

"Pete!" Kate screamed. "What's going on?"

"Herman and Buck are getting away on the freighter," Pete shouted. "They started a fire downstairs but we put it out."

"We?" Eddie asked. His voice came from another part of the black floor.

"Eddie, is that you?" Pete said. "Is everyone all right?"

"Yes, we're okay," Dan said. "We heard footsteps on the stairs and thought Herman was coming to finish us off."

"Hurry!" Ginny said anxiously. "Cut us loose!"

Pete pulled the jackknife from his hip pocket. "I can't see a thing," he said. "Where's the flashlight?"

"Right here," Ginny said. "Behind me."

Pete groped in the dark, felt the heavy object and clicked it on. The room was flooded with light. Pete put his knife to work slashing Kate's bindings. In a few seconds, all were standing with him.

"They were going to burn down the lighthouse," Kate said. "What happened to the fire?"

"And who's this `We' you were talking about?" Eddie persisted.

"It was the strangest thing," Pete said. "I tried to put the flames out by myself, but the heat and smoke were too much. I fell down and suddenly the room got all quiet and still. I was lying there when an old guy wearing a black uniform came out of nowhere with two buckets of water. I asked him if he was the lighthouse keeper. He said he used to be and then doused me with water. Then he showed me where two more pails were kept. We went into a boathouse room and filled the buckets a couple of times and had the fire out in two minutes flat."

Dan glanced outside through the lighthouse window. There, only a hundred yards away, the bow light of the *V.A. Frazier* was moving quickly toward them.

"Hand me the flashlight!" Dan yelled. "Maybe I can signal the captain in Morse code." Dan took the lantern and began a series of long and short flashes to the freighter's bridge. A few seconds passed. He sent the message again.

As the *V.A. Frazier* drew alongside the lighthouse, a brilliant beam blasted into the tower room. Pete and his friends stood out like actors on a Broadway stage. They turned their heads and covered their eyes from the powerful stream of light. The search beam went out and the kids squinted in the darkness. From the *V.A. Frazier's* pilothouse came a softer beacon, blinking a series of pulsing lights.

"They're returning my message!" Dan said.

"What are they saying?" Ginny asked.

"I told them that they were being boarded," Dan said. "They want to know who and where.

"B-u-r-g-l-a-r-s. A-f-t," Dan spelled out in code.

From the pilothouse of the *V.A. Frazier*, Captain Edwards gave the command, "All engines stop!" Suddenly the ship's immense powerhouse became silent. He then ordered, "All engines back!" and quickly sent a series of flashes toward the Coast Guard station on Mackinac Island, "S-O-S, S-u-p-p-o-r-t."

Coast Guard Boat And Station

CHAPTER 29
CAPTURE

"We made it!" Herman LeRoux yelled as he jumped from the boarding ladder to the stern deck of the freighter and joined his comrades, all with smug grins of victory. The two heavy gunnysacks at their sides, their goal was now within reach.

As they stood eagerly awaiting the final phase of their scheme, the thunderous volume of the ship's engine suddenly dropped. The steady throbbing from below ceased. There was a long pause as the *V.A. Frazier* coasted silently under the stars. The three thieves stared blankly at cach othcr. Just as suddenly, an even louder pounding came from the belly of the immense vessel. The entire deck began to shake violently.

"Her engine's full astern!" Sam yelled. "She's stopping!"

"Why? What's going on?" Herman yelled.

Buck pointed toward Mackinac Island. "Over there!" he shouted. "Someone's signaling from the Coast Guard station!"

"What for?" Herman screamed. "They can't be on to us."

Buck turned toward the old lighthouse. "Hey! The fire!" he yelled. "It's out! That kid we couldn't find musta doused it!"

The three jewel smugglers scurried around on the stern deck like scared mice in a cage full of boas.

"Here comes the Coast Guard!" Herman cried.

"Dump the bags!" Buck yelled. "Without the loot, they got nothin' on us. We gotta stay cool. It's our word against that kid's."

Sam and Herman each grabbed a gunnysack, stared at it for a long moment, then pitched it over the rail, shaking their heads.

———

It was still night, but the eastern sky was brightening as the Coast Guard boat pulled up to the shadowy stern of the *V.A. Frazier*. A crowd of curious deck hands stood with the freighter's captain as two state police officers came up the boarding ladder.

"We've got two stowaways," Captain Edwards said to Sergeant Glenn, "plus one of my crew. I knew Sam was up to something. Every time we came near Mackinac, he'd start acting strange. I figured he was signaling a girlfriend or something, but I never dreamed he was doing anything illegal. Take 'em and lock 'em up. I'm behind schedule. With your permission, I'd like to be on my way."

"Permission granted, Captain Edwards," Sergeant Glenn said. "You'll hear from us soon."

The three thieves and the two policemen were lowered from the freighter into the Coast Guard boat. As the *V.A. Frazier* began to move off on her course through the Straits, the smaller Coast Guard craft headed slowly to Round Island. Using its search beam, the vessel's officer brought her close to the gravelly beach. Buck, Herman and Sam remained seated, handcuffed to the stern railing, scanning the shoreline.

They saw five teenagers standing by some tents. Four of them, Kate, Dan, Eddie and Ginny, appeared weary from their captivity, but dry, warm and happy to be alive. Pete Jenkins looked more like a war refugee—and one from the losing side, at that. His face and clothes were blackened with soot and smoke. He was soaked from his jump in the lake and shivering from the northern night's chilly air. But through it all, joy shown through him, knowing that he had saved five lives—including his own—as well as a very old and wonderful lighthouse.

"How did you find these men?" Sergeant Glenn asked the young campers as he jumped from the deck to the shore.

"We didn't find them," Dan explained. "They found us. We thought they had gotten away three days ago and were long gone. We just came over here to camp out for the night." Dan then told Sergeant Glenn how Herman and Buck had tied them in the tower and started the fire in the lighthouse, but that Pete had put it out.

"You got nothin' on us," Buck yelled from the Coast Guard boat. "You can't prove nothin'. Herm an' me just wanted to go for a boat ride with our friend, Sam . . . right Herman? Herm and me, we just love freighters. Sam, too. We all love boats."

"He's right," Sergeant Glenn whispered to his deputy. "With nothing but circumstantial evidence, all we can arrest them for is illegally boarding a commercial vessel—punishable by nothing more than a slap on the wrist. The fire, the kidnapping, the burglaries—it's all these kids' word against theirs."

"When we approached the freighter," Officer Beckman answered quietly, "I saw someone throw two sacks overboard, but I couldn't swear in court who did it. The bags went down like rocks. It's over four hundred feet deep there and the current is too strong to recover them."

"You won't need to," Pete Jenkins said. "What they threw overboard *were* rocks." He opened his tent and

163

pointed inside.

"You got nothin' in there!" Herman yelled from aboard the boat. "You're makin' that up!" He turned to Buck and whispered, "I was in every one of them tents, Buck. Ain't nothin' in 'em. They was all empty. They got nothin'."

"Well, let's just take a look," Sergeant Glenn said. He went to Pete's pup tent and pulled the flap back. He peered into the darkened shelter.

"Give me a light here, Captain," Sergeant Glenn called. The boat's search beam moved across the shoreline. It came to rest on Pete's tent and shone inside upon a dazzling array of gold, silver and jewels. "Well, look what we got here," the policeman shook his head. "I'll bet there's a fingerprint on every one of those pieces. And I wouldn't be a bit surprised if it isn't a perfect match with those of our freighter-loving friends here. What do you say to that, Mr. Meesley?"

Buck Meesley turned ashen as he stared at Pete's gleaming pile of stolen goods. His eyes spoke volumes as he gazed in defeat first at Herman, then at Sam.

"I believe we can now add robbery, arson and attempted murder to that trespassing charge," Sergeant Glenn said to his assistant. He loaded the booty into two canvas bags and handed them to Officer Beckman, who set them in the bow of the Coast Guard boat. He then stepped aboard, turned and faced the five teens. "You're welcome to join us for our ride to Mackinac."

"Thanks, but I think we've shared Herman and Buck's company all we care to for awhile," Kate said. "We'll go back in the *Griffin*."

"That's fine," Sergeant Glenn said. "Just don't get lost. You kids are my star witnesses." He nodded to the Coast Guard captain and the powerful boat churned into the Straits channel.

The Last Farewell

CHAPTER 30
THE FINAL FAREWELL

"Let's pack up," Dan said.

Each camper grabbed a part of what was left of the gear and loaded it into the sailboat.

"Before we leave," Pete said, "we've got to go back to the lighthouse and thank Jesse Muldoon. He saved our lives."

"That's right," Kate said. "Besides, I'd like to meet him. He's probably got some great stories to tell."

"And I want to find out how he's stayed here so long with practically no one ever seeing him," Dan added.

They followed Pete to the charred lighthouse entrance. A fresh breeze had swept most of the smoke from the main room. Pete led the others inside.

"Where is he?" Kate asked.

Pete glanced around. Two empty wooden pails lay on the floor. "I don't know," he said. "He may have gone back to the boat launch room. That's where we got the water to put out the fire."

"We walked through this whole lighthouse

165

yesterday," Kate said. "I don't remember any boat launch room."

Pete stared at a wall where, only an hour before, he had followed Jesse Muldoon to fill the pails. "It's not here," Pete mumbled.

"What are you talking about?" Dan asked.

"The door Mr. Muldoon and I used to fill our buckets. It's not here!" Pete said.

"Did you say, `boat launch room?'" Ginny Lind asked. She backed away from the others toward the scorched entrance.

"Yeah, we sure couldn't go through the front door," Pete said, pointing to the charred remains. "It was a wall of flames."

Ginny moved even closer to the exit. "Last week when you asked me what I knew about Round Island," she said, "I went through our newspaper's files. I found a column my father had written six years ago as the new light station was being built. It seems some vandals came over here in the winter and broke through a boat launch area into the main room. They made a real mess of Mr. Muldoon's quarters. Since the Coast Guard only needed the launching deck to supply the lighthouse for one more season, they decided to seal it up. That door has been boarded over ever since."

"How could that be?" Pete said. "I just went through it an hour ago."

"Maybe I can tell you," Ginny said. "This may be hard to believe, but hear me out. Pete, I don't think you saw Jesse Muldoon last night."

"Sure I did," Pete argued. "It had to be. He even said so."

"No, I think what he told you was that he *used to be* the lighthouse keeper—that *he used to be* Jesse Muldoon. I think what you saw was Jesse Muldoon's

166

ghost. What's more, you didn't just help him put out the fire, Pete. You put it out yourself. Look. There are only two pails here. I'm guessing that both of them are the ones you used to douse the blaze."

"But I saw him," Pete said. "He poured water over me. How could a ghost do that?"

"Oh, he was here, all right," Ginny said. "But he didn't save you by splashing water *on* you. He did it by pouring his spirit *into* you. Remember what Mr. Dufina told you about Tom Willis—the coal dock worker who saw the lights flashing from the lighthouse five years ago? I think what Tom Willis saw that day wasn't just some random reflections off the lighthouse tower. I believe it was Jesse Muldoon's signal that his life was flickering out. I think he died that day, but I believe his spirit remained here, so that even in death, he could guard his lighthouse, just as he had in person, all his life. It was his bullheaded spirit that the ghost poured into you as you lay on the floor. Don't you see? He *couldn't* let you die. Only *you* could save his lighthouse."

Pete shook his head, not wanting to believe it. He shuddered as the idea sank in. He began to nod. "Maybe that's why, when he poured the water on me, it didn't feel cold and wet —but soft and warm. And why each time he dumped his pails on the fire, nothing happened," Pete whispered. "It was only when I followed him that the flames went out."

The five friends stared for a moment at the boarded-up wall, then moved from the smoke-fouled room out into the sweet fragrance of fresh Mackinac air. They walked to the *Griffin* and quickly shoved off.

The black of night gradually gone way to the grey of dawn as Dan hoisted the mainsail. Kate and Ginny set the jib and Pete pushed the centerboard into place. A warm breeze dried Pete's damp clothes as the *Griffin* skimmed across the shipping channel.

While the others kept their eyes ahead on Mackinac harbor, Pete stared wistfully toward Round Island and the beautiful old lighthouse that had almost been destroyed.

Suddenly, as the sun broke over the eastern horizon, a flash of brilliant light came from the lighthouse tower. It shone directly upon the *Griffin*.

"Look!" shouted Pete.

The others turned to see where Pete was pointing. Each caught a glimpse of the blinding light before it dimmed.

"It's only the sun reflecting off the glass," Dan said.

A moment later, the beacon again blazed from the lighthouse, its beam shining a full three seconds directly upon the small sloop. The five sailors stared in amazement, shielding their eyes from the brilliance, until the light went out. Again, it went on and remained steady for another three seconds. The three long flashes were quickly followed by two short bursts of intense, pure white light.

"There's no way the sun could be doing *that*," Dan gasped.

"Three longs and two shorts," Eddie whispered, "that's how sailors greet each other at sea."

Pete stood and waved toward the tower. "This time it means something more," he said. "Unless I miss my guess, that was the last salute anyone will ever see from the Ghost of Round Island Light."

SUGGESTIONS FOR PARENTS AND TEACHERS
by Edna C. Stephens - Educational Consultant

The following activities were designed to extend the ideas and concepts presented in the story. *Permission is given to duplicate CONNECT-IT™ learning activities for non-commercial individual or classroom use only.*

BEFORE READING: Help children set a purpose for reading or listening by having them look at the cover of the book, read the title and predict what they think the story will be about. Ask:
- What is an island?
- Where is the Round Island Lighthouse?
- Have you ever been to Mackinac Island?
- Have you visited any other island?
- Have you ever seen or visited a lighthouse?
- Why are lighthouses important? Etc.

DURING READING: Stop at important parts of the story and ask: *What do you think will happen next?* or *Do you think the children will find the thief? Why or Why not?* Etc.

AFTER READING: Ask important questions, questions that encourage children to think about and reflect on what they have read or heard.

You may wish to have children:
- tell, write or draw the part they liked best in the story.
- tell, write or draw something they were surprised to learn about in the story.
- write or tell at least three things they learned in the story. Example: *British Landing is where British troops came ashore in a sneak attack on the Americans at Fort Mackinac in 1812.*
- research the history of the Grand Hotel on Mackinac Island.
- research the history of Fort Mackinac.
- read the *Beacon of Light: Lighthouses* by Gail Gibbons.
- research the number and locations of lighthouses in Michigan.
- locate the following on a Michigan map and write the map coordinates and county, when appropriate:

Cheboygan	Straits of Mackinac	Detour
Sault Ste. Marie	Les Cheneaux Islands	Mackinac Island

- research the different types of freighters on the Great Lakes.
- calculate the number of miles from their home or school to:

Mackinac Island	Chicago	Cincinnati

- write at least four important questions for each chapter and write four multiple-choice answers (A-D). Combine all the questions to make a Trivia Game. (Each student would be assigned one chapter.) Divide the class into two teams, read the questions and have the team take turns answering the questions. The team who answers the most questions wins!

VOCABULARY PUZZLE

Solve the puzzle to find the answer to the lighthouse riddle.

In the box are vocabulary words from the *Mystery at Round Island Light*. Match the word with its definition. Copy the letters in each numbered box into the matching box of the answer.

A. melancholy	D. schooner	G. scabbard	J. Cockney
B. stowaway	E. dinghy	H. seance	K. hammock
C. derelict	F. vagrant	I. windfall	L. unintelligible

1. Understanding is difficult or impossible.

   `[ ][26][ ][ ][6][ ][ ][ ][ ][ ][ ][ ][29]`

2. A dialect or accent of the natives of the East End of London.

   `[27][21][ ][ ][30][3][ ]`

3. A small open boat carried by a bigger boat to be used as a lifeboat or pleasure boat.

   `[17][ ][13][ ][23][ ]`

4. A sheath or cover for a dagger or sword.

   `[9][ ][ ][ ][ ][ ][ ][ ]`

5. A sailing vessel having at least two masts.

   `[ ][ ][7][15][33][16][18][19]`

6. A hanging length of canvas hung between two trees and used as a seat or bed.

   `[ ][ ][ ][ ][ ][4][ ][ ]`

7. A sudden, unexpected piece of good fortune or personal gain.

   `[ ][28][2][ ][5][ ][ ][ ]`

8. One who wanders from place to place without a permanent home or means of livelihood.

   `[11][ ][ ][ ][ ][ ][31]`

9. Sadness or depression of the spirits: gloom.

   `[ ][10][ ][25][ ][ ][ ][ ][35][ ]`

10. Neglectful of duty, responsibility or obligation.

    `[36][8][34][ ][ ][ ][ ][ ]`

11. A meeting of people to receive messages from spirits.

    `[20][12][ ][ ][ ][24]`

12. A person who hides aboard a ship in order to obtain free passage.

    `[ ][22][1][14][ ][32][ ][ ]`

LIGHTHOUSE RIDDLE: The first lighthouse located at Alexandria used a fire as its light and was also...

`[1][2][3] [4][5] [6][7][8] [9][10][11][12][13] [14][15][16][17][18][19][20]`

`[21][5] [22][23][24] [25][26][27][28][29][30][31] [32][33][34][35][36]`

MAKE A MINI-BOOK

Follow the directions below to make a MINI-BOOK.
Use your book for one of the following:

1. Write the TITLE of the book on the cover.
   Label the pages with the <u>five</u> <u>Story</u> <u>Elements</u>:
   <u>Characters, Setting, Problem(s), Solution, Ending</u>
   and <u>retell</u> the story. Draw pictures for each page
   and write your <u>favorite</u> <u>part</u> of the story on the
   <u>back cover</u>.
2. Label each page with the name of one of the
   characters in the story. Write at least three
   important facts about each one and a question
   you would like to ask them.
3. Write the name of a <u>Mackinac Island landmark</u> on
   each page and list three facts about each one.
4. Research and write about the history of the
   <u>Round Island Lighthouse</u>.
5. Label each page with the name of a different
   <u>Michigan lighthouse</u>. Draw a picture and write the
   location and facts about each one.
6. Label each page with the name of an <u>island found
   in Great Lakes</u>. Write a paragraph about each one.
7. Write about events from <u>Mackinac Island's history</u>.
   Use a 12" x 18" sheet of construction paper.

1. Fold paper into eights. Open.	2. Fold in half.
3. Cut 1/2 way down middle.	4. Fold in half lengthwise.
5. Push ends together.	6. Fold to make a book.

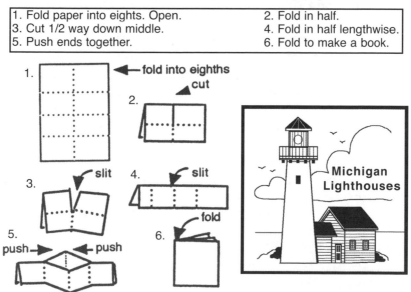

MAKE A STORY HOUSE

Use a 12" x 18" sheet of construction paper.

1. Fold paper into fourths. Open.
2. Fold in half again.
3. Fold flaps in to meet at the center.
4. Pull flaps apart. Push down on the triangle to form doors and a roof.

Push down on the triangle.

Push flaps apart.

Suggestions for your STORY HOUSE ...

1. Make the house into Anderson's cottage or the old shed. Open the doors and draw <u>characters</u> from the story.

2. <u>Retell</u> the story or tell your favorite part of the story on writing paper. <u>Glue</u> it inside the house.

3. Draw the <u>characters</u> inside the house. <u>Color</u> and <u>glue</u> the house onto a 12"x18" paper and draw the <u>setting</u> of the story around the house. <u>Retell</u> the story on the back of the paper.

4. On the roof, write the <u>title</u> of the story. Label each of the four flaps: SETTING, PROBLEM, SOLUTION, ENDING. Open the doors and write CHARACTERS. Fill in the information for the story under the label. Draw the <u>characters</u> inside the doors. <u>Lift</u> <u>the</u> <u>front</u> of the house and retell the story on the <u>inside</u>.

5. Use this STORY HOUSE to write about another Mackinac Island adventure with Kate, Pete, Eddie, Dan and Ginny.

CONNECT-IT™

MAKE A LIGHTHOUSE

The shape of a lighthouse can be made from these familiar geometric solids.

- •cylinder
- •cone
- •cube
- •rectangular box
- •square pyramid

Make a model of a lighthouse using geometry!
Materials: (See diagram on the next page)

- •paper cup
- •half-pint milk cartons
- •paper tube
- •8" paper plate
- •paper
- •stiff cellophane

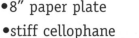 

1. Use a circular plate for the island.
2. A large paper cup turned upside down will make the tower in the shape of a truncated cone.
3. To form the cylinder of the lantern, use a piece of paper tube with rectangles cut out for the lighthouse beam to show through.
4. Glue stiff cellophane behind rectangles.
5. Make a roof using a circle of paper that is cut on its radius and curled into a cone.
6. An empty, half-pint milk carton makes a great light keeper's house.
7. Use construction paper, paint and glue to finish your model.
8. Paint the paper plate with glue and sprinkle it with sand.
9. Decorate the model with small pebbles and twigs.
10. Crumpled plastic wrap makes great waves dashing against your island.

LIGHT UP YOUR LIGHTHOUSE

Find out how a light source works. Light up your
lighthouse! You will need the following materials:
- unassembled lighthouse model
- small flashlight-size bulb
- 2 insulated copper wires (12" long)
- D cell battery

Procedure:
1. Punch a small hole in the paper plate in the center
   of the spot where the lighthouse will sit.
2. Strip about an inch of the coating off of the copper
   wires.
3. Attach one end of each copper wire to the bulb
   using tape.
4. Punch a hole in the lantern floor (bottom of the
   paper cup) large enough to nestle the bulb.
5. Thread the wires through the tower then pass them
   through the hole in the plate.
6. Secure the lighthouse tower to the plate with glue.
7. Attach the battery under the paper plate using tape.
8. Finish decorating.
9. To light up the lighthouse, tape the wire ends to the
   battery terminals.

*Adapted from Lighthouse Builders Need to Know Math
http://groton.k12.ct.us/www/ct/math/html

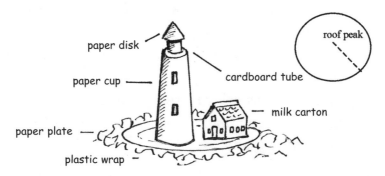

FOLD-and-CUT CHARACTER

Follow the directions below to make Pete and Kate or other characters in the *Mystery at Round Island Light*.

Use a 12″ x 18″ sheet of construction paper.

1. Fold the paper into eighths. Open. (See illustration.)
2. Cut out sections 5 and 8 and save for the arms.
3. Fold sections 1 and 4 toward the center. Fold the top corners back to make a collar.
4. Glue on arms.
5. Make head, hair, hands and feet from other pieces of paper and glue to your character.
6. Dress your characters appropriately.

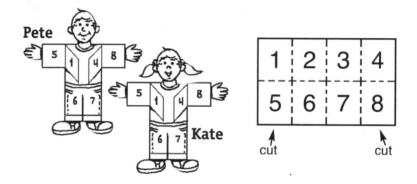

WHAT YOU CAN DO WITH THE CHARACTER:

- Write some important facts about the character on writing paper and glue inside the shirt.
- Tell the story from the character's point of view.
- Glue your character to a large piece of poster board. Draw or find pictures in old magazines that relate to the story. Glue them to the poster board and write a sentence for each picture. Example: <u>dinghy</u> - *The kids took Mr. Anderson's <u>dinghy</u> to Round Island.*
- Use your character as a prop for an oral book report.
- Make the character into yourself and tell which part of the story you liked best.

CONNECT-IT™

Other Books By Robert A. Lytle

Mackinac Passage: A Summer Adventure

Fifteen-year-old Pete Jenkins meets two boys and a girl near his summer cabin in northern Michigan. The new friends find clues linking a hermit writer to a counterfeit money scheme. Setting aside other activities for the intrigue of spying, they follow the elderly man by sail to nearby Mackinac Island. To their horror, the tale turns to one of murder. A test of wills leads them through a series of terrifying obstacles to a remarkable conclusion. 178 pages

Mackinac Passage: The Boathouse Mystery

Fifteen-year-old Pete Jenkins and his three summer friends return to their cottages following a perilous escapade on nearby Mackinac Island. They soon learn that many boathouses in the Les Cheneaux Islands resort community are being looted - theirs included. Curiosity prevails and the teens investigate. Unknown to them, however, the escaped Mackinac murderer lurks in the shadows plotting a fiendish scheme of revenge. 176 pages

Mackinac Passage: The General's Treasure

As a reward for their heroics, fifteen-year-old Pete Jenkins and his three Cincinnati Row friends revisit the Andersons at their magnificent cottage on Mackinac Island. Pete's idea of rest and relaxation is soon interrupted by a chance meeting with an elderly heiress. She presents Pete with a seemingly worthless poem which leads the inquisitive teens to various sites around the Island - and ultimately into the perilous grasp of a deranged treasure hunter. 172 pages

Three Rivers Crossing

Walker Morrison, a modern-day, thirteen-year-old boy, goes fly-fishing near his home in Rochester, Michigan. Suddenly trapped underwater, he awakens to find himself on the bank of the river 180 years in the past, rescued by his own great-great-great-great grandfather. Walker reveals his secret to another boy, Daniel Taylor, his great-great-great-granduncle, and together they work to return Walker to his own time. In the meantime, he learns to adapt to living on the frontier in the 1820s with his new family. 161 pages

A Pitch In Time

Tells the tale of a modern day boy who tumbles from his bike and wakes up to find he has traveled back in time to the spring of 1864 in rural Michigan during the Civil War. His southern accent, cultural views and even the sport he loves all come in conflict with everything he has ever known. The story unfolds as his new 19th century friend, Sally Norton, helps him learn the ways of a war-torn Northern community. 316 pages

COMING SOON ...

Mackinac Passage: Pirate Party

It's late August, 1952. Fifteen-year-old Pete Jenkins joins his resort friends for an end-of-summer party. Dressed in pirate outfits, they board a small but sturdy craft and head off to an uninhabited island for picnic and prizes—all provided for by Mr. Heuck, a Captain Hook-like cottager. In the distance Pete, Kate and Dan spy an antique, three-masted schooner. They rush out to greet it, but rather than simply waving hello to a bunch of history buffs, they are invited aboard. The three soon find themselves captive and part of an enormous fleet of British, Canadian and Indian attackers bent on taking over Fort Mackinac. They discover that the performers are in fact, real invaders bent on returning the newly established United States of America back into English hands. Their make-believe social gathering in 1952 has become a real-life battle for survival in the War of 1812. 184 pages

**To order, call EDCO at 888-510-3326
or visit us at www.edcopublishing.com**

**2648 Lapeer Rd
Auburn Hills, MI 48326**

About the Author:
In the olden days in Ireland and the Scottish Highlands, the seanachie (*sen-ah-key*, the teller of tales) was welcomed with all the excitement and enthusiasm of today's rock stars: The seanachie was treated with honor and respect—for he was one who passed down the traditions and history of the Celtic peoples—sagas we would today call myths, legends, or even fairy tales.

Young readers are fortunate to have a modern-day seanachie in Robert Lytle, an award-winning Michigan author who brings his Michigan childhood experiences to life in his books.

When he was five years old his family came into possession of a crude but habitable cabin in the Les Cheneaux Islands of Michigan's upper peninsula. Every summer thereafter was filled with sunny days spent fishing, sailing, swimming, hiking and exploring. During his summer breaks from Ferris State, where he was studying to become a pharmacist, Bob worked on Mackinac Island as a dock porter at the Island House Hotel, as a dockmaster at the yacht dock and as a folk singer at the Lake View Hotel. It was here he met his future wife in his last Mackinac summer.

He wouldn't know how important his time spent in northern Michigan would be to his writings for many decades. Graduation from pharmacy school, marriage, a "real" job and a new family, which grew to include four sons, called him away from northern Michigan for 25 years.

Robert published his first book in 1995. His first two works were selected by the Great Lakes Booksellers Association to be included in their list of the "Top Ten Children's Books of the Year." He continues to write every day.

The tradition of the seanachie has all but died out—but here and there around the globe, it survives, kept alive and carried on by the imagination and talent of a master tale-spinner. When not actively writing or working in his store, Bob enjoys visiting schools to discuss his stories, history, music and like the ancient seanachie, telling stories to enthralled young people of all ages.

About the Illustrator:
Karen Howell, Bob's sister, is also a lifetime enthusiast of Michigan's history and natural beauty. Her award-winning art can be found in many galleries and homes throughout Michigan. A former dental hygienist and an avid Great Lakes sailor she now dedicates much of her time to her art—and to her many grandchildren.